GIPSY FLOWER

Noah was a member of one of the gipsy tribes which came every year to the fair in the village field. It was there he fell in love with Fay, the shepherd's daughter. It was fate that brought about their romantic meeting in the old barn which smelled so sweetly of a forgotten summer; it was fate also that sent Richard, the big theatrical producer, to them. He promised fame to Noah, so that he could defy the opposition of the tribes and the village and marry Fay. Noah left her, promising that he would return next fair day.

   This is a story of village life and of the roads along which the gipsy vans turn their yellow wheels, a love story full of colour and romance.

GIPSY FLOWER

By Ursula Bloom

Again I saw a brown bird hover
Over the flowers at my feet;
I felt a brown bird hover
Over my heart and sweet.
Its shadow lay on my heart.
I thought I saw on the clover
A brown bee pulling apart
The closed flesh of the clover
And burrowing in its heart.

D. H. LAWRENCE

ROBERT HALE · LONDON

First published in Great Britain 1949

This edition 1984

ISBN 0 7090 1627 1

Robert Hale Limited
Clerkenwell House
Clerkenwell Green
London EC1R 0HT

For

ALICE NASH

Who was always so very appreciative

Printed in Great Britain by
Photobooks (Bristol) Ltd.
and bound by
W.B.C. Bookbinders Ltd.

PART ONE

INTRODUCTION

The full streams feed on flower of rushes,
  Ripe grasses trammel a travelling foot,
The faint fresh flame of the young year flushes
  From leaf to flower, and flower to fruit:
And fruit and leaf are as gold and fire,
And the oat is heard above the lyre,
And the hoofèd heel of a satyr crushes
The chestnut bark at the chestnut root.

SWINBURNE.

I

ALL the winter the gipsies did not stir, but
stayed in their caravans, and came out only to
search for wood, or to snare rabbits, or to beg.
They stacked their caravans shoulder to shoulder in the little valley protected from the worst
winds and rains. Storm did not penetrate their
hideout.

And with the spring they came out again, to
sell their pegs, to tell their fortunes, and to
snare, and beg, and sometimes to pilfer.

Old Haidee did not hold with pilfering. She
was of the clan of true gipsy which is dead
honest, and she complained that mixed blood
had brought evil-doers to her tribe. They had
wed unwisely, and not in the manner of the true
gipsy who looks to Romany maid, and is not to

be persuaded from dark eyes, and the barefoot walk which is the true gipsy.

Later, when the summer first breathed warmly, the vans would come out of their winter stronghold, and would form a procession. Haidee led, in hers. She was queen of the gipsies, old and wrinkled, with fine brass rings in her ears, and gold chains snapped with large smooth corals at her throat, and a fine white lace apron. She was fit to be queen, and wise with her years. No man knew her exact age, even her three sons, and her two daughters, and the sons-in-law and the daughters-in-law, and the children who came after them.

She was old, with dark furtive eyes, and black hair raddled with silver in places but still showing that rich, lustrous darkness born of Romany.

They would take to the road again, this long raggle-taggle procession, with the lean horses, the little piebald ponies, the vans themselves with yellow and red wheels, and the little carts which take the clothes pegs and the rag mats for sale, and the lavender baskets. In between the wheels the lurchers would run, and when they got away from the towns, and out into the countryside again, the lurchers would take one each side of a hedge, for they knew their work was to find dinner for the gipsies.

The procession always started the week before Epsom, and went straight to the downs. Here, if they had a good day, they laid in store for the next winter. People were in amiable moods; they could be bribed to have their hands told, they would pay for the tip which (the gipsies always vowed in their soothing, sweet-as-honey tones) had been given them by a jockey who knew. They would be tempted into spending more than they meant.

"A bit of white heather, sir; it'll bring you luck."

"A penny, pretty lady, a penny for the baby."

"Tell your fortune; you've got a lucky hand, you've got a lucky life. You'll be lucky in love, dear, but beware of a dark man. . . ."

All the old jargon, and the fools believed it!

Not one in ten of the gipsies could tell truly, and they knew it. Haidee could see things. But that sight which peers into the future is not given to all, though what did it matter if the gullible public thought that it was?

And after Epsom came other race courses, and finally the hop fields in Kent, where the gipsies always worked away from the others because they did not mix with the ragtag. They also refused to sleep in hoppers huts, but would take a corner of their field for their vans and stay there with their own little community speaking their own tongue.

Much later, when the berries came and the cold nights, they would come back to the valley hemmed in with trees, and settle themselves for the winter.

The wood smoke of their fires would rise again, and the sound of the men chopping at pegs, and of the girls in a rage calling to their children, and of old Haidee screaming at those who had married yellowheads and village girls, who were not of the clan.

There they would stay till the next season.

II

SOMETIMES it was fairs that they would be visiting. There was a cocoanut shy or two in the back van, and Haidee would tell fortunes again, and there was a hoop-la with a great box of cheap prizes and rings which never did fit the stands, though of course they argued that they did.

Old Haidee had her caravan set in a prominent place, and Tessa, who was the most persuasive of her children and who could be relied

upon to waft people up the steps and in at
the highly painted door—Tessa knew how to
play on superstitions. She was a big brawny
girl with piercing black eyes and thick black
hair.

But of all her children, probably Haidee
loved Noah the most. He had been born long
after she had supposed that child-bearing days
were over. Her family was growing up, stalwart
and strong, and the boys were lean youths who
could be relied upon to snare a rabbit or to
wheedle money from passers-by. Zilla was married, with a fat babe tied to her in a shawl; the
boy had been born in time for Epsom, and had
made them a tidy sum on the downs, where they
had exploited him. "A penny for the baby,
lady; a penny for the baby."

Then Noah was born.

A month before he was due, the father died.
He was an old man, and his heart had played
tricks on him. It was in the winter too, a hard
winter, with little saved and times bad. That
year they had had troubles because there had
been difficulties at the hopping fields, when a
band of tinkers had set upon the vans and had
robbed them. The gipsies and the tinkers were
always at variance, and could never be relied
upon to dwell together. Usually the gipsies

won every squabble, but this time the tinkers did well.

The result was that the winter was hard. The trade in clothes pegs was not good, and people did not seem to wish to buy the feather brooms and the old mats which the girls took from door to door.

Haidee ruled her subjects with a will of iron, and promised them better things for the summer. She could see them in her crystal.

"Do you really see in that thing?" Noah asked her.

She told him because he was the child of her heart, the only one that she would have told. In the crystal often there was nothing but cloud, and bewilderment, and a density which her eyes could not penetrate, but sometimes there was clarity, and a star, or people moving, or hope, or good luck, or love. Of course when she told crystals for the silly, credulous people who flocked round the caravan at fairs, or who came across the hop fields to seek her out where she was picking, or for the village girls who came surreptitiously to her tent, then she told the story she thought that they would like to hear. Nobody gave a thank-you for unhappy predictions; they wanted to learn of tall dark strangers who would bring them joy, of money coming, and letters of good fortune. She had to judge her client, and tell the story she thought might be suitable. She never even bothered to search in the crystal then.

"I see," said Noah.

"I tell you because you are my son, my own son!"

"But my brothers."

She shook her head. "They were never sons as you are my son. Neither are Tessa and Zilla my daughters as you are mine. In every brood there is one beloved." She turned her fine bright eyes upon him. "You are my beloved, Noah."

He caught her hand and pressed it. It was a well-bred hand, no working woman's hand, even though it might be stained from hopping, and with calluses from hard work. But there was royal blood behind Haidee, and that same blood ran in his veins too.

"One day," she said, "I shall look in my crystal and see your bride walking into it. She will be dark-skinned, and with black hair, and bright eyes. I shall know her when I see her. No fair-haired girl for my Noah. No turning from his own clan."

He said nothing. He, for his part, had a cleaving to golden hair, and that mayblossom complexion of some of the girls who came to his mother's tent and asked for their futures. He would not have dared to tell her.

She said: " Don't think that there is anything you can keep from me, my son, because there is not. Not whilst I have my crystal."

"There'll never be anything to keep from you."

She said: "I know."

He did not know why the thought made him unhappy.

THE FAIR

No sweeter sight is ever seen
Than swings upon a village green,
No sweeter sound than laughter gay
And crowds, and all the roundelay
Which come from far and wide, and there
Forget all but the village fair.

Anon.

I

THE first of the fairs was Easter week, on a wide common in a Kentish village just beyond London. Because the year had been so bad, and there had been trouble with the tinkers again last autumn, the gipsies decided to come to the fair, hoping to have a lucky day. The main bulk of the caravans would stay behind, but three of them would come, and the two gay little light carts with the cocoanut shies, and the hoopla with the faulty rings, and the shooting booth that Tessa sometimes managed, with improperly sighted rifles that made it so difficult even for crack shots to get a prize.

"Try your luck, gentlemen; walk up and try your luck!" Her raucous voice never tired, and she would stand there from midday, when the fair opened, until after midnight, screaming to passers-by to have a shot and win a prize.

It was an early Easter, and surprisingly mild, as the vans turned out of their valley and took the Kent road towards the common just out of London.

Noah was driving Haidee's van; she had insisted upon coming because she and her crystal were a greater draw than anything else that the gipsies could provide. She lounged over the open window, chatting to Noah and eyeing the weather, with its April sky of pale blue and its cirrus of cottonwool clouds. The willow was in blossom, and there were the first signs of green upon the trees, with their thickening branches, and the birds were singing.

"And another hard winter to come," said Haidee, surveying all the signs which meant nothing to the average man but everything to her. She could read the weather months ahead from the hedgerows and the fields, and the way that the river chuckled amongst its stones.

"When shall I ever know all that you know?" he asked.

"Some day! These things are given to the gipsies," she answered.

The horse moved slowly, with a pleasant clopping, like drumming. There was the sound of the wheels rotating through the little dusty lane, for they did not use the highways more than was necessary, seeing that the lanes might lend them a rabbit or rarer game, if the going was good.

He said: "There has always been a tie between us, you and me, hasn't there? More than with the others."

And she answered, "Yes, more than with the others," surveying him proudly, her bright eyes shining as she rammed the tobacco down into the bowl of her short clay pipe.

"It'll always be like this?" he ventured.

She said: "No, not always like this. I know today we are going to something new. Something different. We shall see strange folk, and you'll see a strange face. But although for a time it will seem to come between us, the trouble will pass."

He did not know what she meant.

"I'll not be making trouble," he said, but uneasily, for he remembered his love of soft fair hair, and his longing for it at times.

"You'll be making trouble sure enough"; and she laughed. "It is a trouble all women have to bear with their sons if they love them very well."

"You're talking in riddles."

She shook her head.

"No. I'm talking sense. When a mother loves her son, she loves him differently from the way that she thinks of a daughter. It's a jealous love. She hates the girl who takes him from her, because her love is a love that can be hurt that way. Few women hate their sons-in-law, but all women feel jealous of their daughters-in-law. That's life! You'll hurt me more than any of the others have been able to hurt me, because I love you more."

"I don't want to hurt you," he said doggedly.

She said, "No, but you'll hurt me just the same," and then as she lit the pipe, and leaned her brown fine hands upon the low doorway, staring out at the lane and puffing at the pipe, she said, "Sing to me."

Noah had a beautiful voice.

The others sang raucously. They had the gipsy voices which sing the lavender song through the London streets on an August afternoon, the sweet, mocking song which is taught from mother to child, and is sung hoarsely, with throats like brass. But Noah had a throat that was made of glass. Once, when he had been only a lad, a strange man had come to the caravans because he had heard Noah singing. He had spoken to old Haidee about him.

"That boy could be trained to something exceptional," he said.

Old Haidee had hoped that was a chance to

make money and had immediately suggested that something on account would help towards the training. The man had met gipsies before, and he was not listening to her. He wanted to take Noah to some classes of his own, which, of course, was just a piece of nonsense, as she agreed.

She was not having anything like that.

At the time they had laughed at it, and had been amused at the way the man had made off, with the lurchers under the vans straining at their leads and barking after him. They did not want any of his sort round the place.

Noah had gone on singing. He sang because life was good, and he loved the flowers, and the lanes, and the rain which came in April and the sun which came in May, and the corn with September, when the earth itself was warmed through and hot to the touch.

He sang now, and she listened to him. His voice was tender as a woman's. It had none of the hoarseness of Tessa or Zilla, but reminded her of the nightingale which on a late spring evening she sometimes listened to in the valleys beyond Epsom. The nightingale was the most beautiful of all the birds, and even Haidee would stop to listen to him. Indescribable, she thought, and very like Noah, who sang as though water gurgled in his throat, as though he walked high mountains, or felt that it was always spring.

So the van passed out of the lane, into the main road which led towards London and where the cars sped to and fro. It had started out on the first trek of the year.

II

THEY came to the village when it was almost evening. It was situated in a valley just off the main road, with a high hill rising behind it, where the scabious grew in summer, and where now the primroses were pushing upwards and lifting pale little faces to the sky. On the common there were the dried bleached grasses of last year, and the blackberry bushes tired with winter, and the darkness of gorse to which a torch had been set, for in places it blossomed goldly.

Other entertainers were already on the scene, and the place was active and alive with men hammering up stands. There were Bert Rigby's galloping horses in the main position as they deserved. There was a long thin line of side shows, shies, and rifle ranges, and fat ladies and the dwarfs. For the moment everybody was busy with scaffolding, and whilst the men worked with their hard wooden mallets, the children from the village rushed about or stood in groups watching.

" Here come the gipsies," somebody called, and instantly the youngest children began to cry, for their mothers told them that gipsies stole little children, and they believed it even in modern days.

The vans came down the roadway, to their pitch at the far corner. Almost at once the horses were unharnessed and set free to graze, and the men got busy with the stands. Haidee was working amongst them, urging them to make haste. She did not believe in laziness, and was always behind them to belabour them if they were too slow. The stands were up in a short time because of her insistency.

The days died young, for the spring was still immature, and she wanted to see everything in place before nightfall.

Long before the daylight dimmed into saffron and pale pink in the west, and the first stars came perking through the sky, the scaffolding was in place, and the tawdry striped awnings with their staggering announcements written across them were pulled over and knotted into place. The cocoanut stands stood in empty wire knots. The hoop-la was spread with its square little blocks, like a table all ready to be set with the viands for offer. Then, and only then, did Haidee consent to have their evening meal, with the chilliness of night blowing across the common, so that some of them brought down shawls and sat in them around the fire.

The men went off, for tomorrow they would be up betimes and it would mean that no food could be got. There was the larder to be replenished tonight. They took the dogs and went to the wild fields beyond the village and stretching over the hill. There was a small plantation there which had been kind to them before. Noah went with them.

They came back quite silently a couple of hours later, the dogs tiredly, their jaws stained with blood, the men with apparently nothing, but their pockets full. They slung themselves into their places saying never a word.

Haidee lay in her bunk, and she stared out at the stars through the open doorway. She saw in them destiny that was written for her and for hers. She knew quite well that the hour had come when she would be facing difficulty and trial, and that she had got to face it bravely. She was unafraid. All her life she had been courageous, from that time when she was born a muling bit of a babe in this same caravan which had been her mother's before her; through the years when she had learnt to rule her people with that iron will, and to steer them through hard times.

She thought, impatiently, this hour would never have been if only she had not loved too well, because she did love Noah better than all the others, and because of that love would suffer more for him.

She did not sleep.

She lay there listening to the horses stirring, to Zilla in the next van quarrelling with her husband, to the dogs on chain below the vans, the rasping and the shuffling, and beyond them all those myriad sounds of the night world when wild creatures hunt.

Tomorrow, she knew, something would happen.

III

Come, come,
Come to the fair. . . .

Song.

IT was a fine day.

She had known it would be fine when she had looked across the narrow doorway of her van and had watched the sun set, with that pinkish glow which bodes ill at morning but well at night.

She dressed herself, and listened to Noah singing as he went amongst the horses. This was a
day for finery, and she tied a multicoloured
scarf round her throat and put on her coral and
gold necklace, the bridal one in which she had
been married, and the apron with the lace
around it, a heavy coarse lace that she was
proud of. In her ears she hung her best chandelier earrings, the kind that had been her
grandmother's and were handed on. But these
earrings would never go to Tessa or Zilla; she
would give them to Noah's wife, because Noah
would be king after her and his wife would be
queen.

She had arranged that in her own mind.

Already Zilla was setting out the hoop-la, with
the real gold watches they had bought at so
much a gross displayed with lavish notices. The
men were busy with the cocoanuts, and there
were mugs of tea to be had.

There was little time this morning to tidy the
vans, because now everything concentrated on
the business of the day, save for Haidee's van,
with its polished stove, and its fine lace, and its
gay colours. The bunk was spread as though
for a wedding, and she looked upon it with
pride. So many village girls who came in here
for their fortunes to be told expressed surprise

at the beauty of her van and the fineness of her belongings. They thought that gipsies were poor creatures, who lived dirtily, and in whose vans there were not even the necessities of life; they confused them with the tinkers, who were very different folk.

There was nothing in Haidee's van that was not polished and shining, nothing that was not of the best.

And she in her bridal finery sitting at the doorway, waiting for some village lover to be tempted up the steps, for his or her fortune to be told in the crystal.

"A fine fortune today, my pretty; a fine fortune, and a handsome husband. Listen to what the gipsy tells you, because she tells truly."

All the old jargon!

At midday Bert Rigby's galloping horses started their raucous music, churning out tunes of a couple of years ago, and the plaster figures in front of the gilt pipes began to wag their silly heads, and to beat their stupid cymbals, and make manifestations as though this were the greatest fun in the world. The little cars began to spin, and the horses (for the more venturesome) went up and down on their brass poles. They were yellow spotted with the sun-yellow that Haidee loved best, and they were gaudy; in fact they were most fantastic horses, though she would never have recognized that fact.

Noah was at the hoop-la.

She had the feeling that she ought to be watching him, but it was not possible, for already the first couple of silly twittering girls were on the steps of the caravan, eyeing her apprehensively, half afraid. They had to be encouraged. She leaned down to them.

"Come, my pretties, come; no need to be afraid. The gipsy only wants to help you. It's trouble with that young man of yours, isn't it? He isn't the one for you. Oh, I know how you feel; come and talk to the old gipsy and she'll tell you what is the right thing to do."

And she had them up the steps, awkward-looking girls, nudging one another, and half afraid to speak. She had them sitting opposite to her, whilst she peered into the crystal, clouded and showing her nothing at all, but it made a good impression on the onlookers who could see her through the van window, and who thought it was clever.

"And she tells true, she does," said one woman to another. "She told my Nell only the year before last, 'You'll be the mother of two,' she said, and two it was. A boy and a girl. Pigeon pair, and she as proud as could be."

Noah stood lounging against a pole of the hoop-la proffering his rings.

"Four for threepence. Try your luck. Four for threepence and a prize every time. A prize for every one you cover. Four for threepence."

He ignored the fact that it was almost quite impossible to cover any of the rings, however hard you tried. Zilla was calling the other side. Her voice was raucous and she could make it carry. But he would rather have his own voice, like the nightingale, so his mother said, but mellow and tender, and of immense compass.

Then he saw the girl.

He was used to girls at fairs, for most of his time he seemed to be coming into contact with them. They were so many silly sheep, who came to waste their money on fritterings which were no use to them. This girl was not like that. She stood away from the others, smallish, and lightly boned. She had not the wide hips and the brave breasts of gipsy girls, who are made to stride through the rain and the snow, and not to feel the harshness of the world into which they are cast.

This girl was lovely. Her face was small and pointed, and very pale. Like a cuckoo smock,

he thought, white with that translucent shade
upon it, and her mouth was like a rosy flower
crushed into that whiteness. Her eyes were
blue. They were not that dark blue which
some of the gipsies can show, but pale again,
like the little harebells which come in July and
grow on dry soil only. There was none of the
blueness of the spring bluebells in those eyes,
he thought, but everything that was pale to
match her skin. Her hair was gold. That also
was pale. It was the exquisite pallor which
attracted him, seeing that he himself was so
darkly brown, and with such large black eyes
and so tawny a head.

He flung down the rings. Somebody else
could carry on with them, he told himself; they
did not matter any more!

He advanced to where the girl was standing,
her hands thrust into the wide pockets of her
old rough coat, staring at the van where Haidee
was telling fortunes. Haidee's head could be
seen through the small square of window, bent
over the hand of some village girl, whose friend
lingered awkwardly on the steps as though
afraid to go inside.

Noah was so used to the background of fair,
of hoop-la, and cocoanut shy, and perhaps most
of all the van where Haidee told fortunes, that

he noticed nothing unusual about it; but he did notice something unusual about the girl with the pale gold hair and the mayblossom skin, like hawthorn in the hedges of mid-spring.

He said, " Getting your fortune told?" because it was the only query he could think of. " She tells true. She tells of things to come, and it helps to know. Maybe it is riches you want, or a lover, or a fine house?"

And he grinned. He had even white teeth, teeth which had never been cleaned in his life because he did not hold with that sort of thing, but teeth which kept themselves clean because they were so used to the nuts, and the berries, and the little hard crab apples which he got from the hedges. The girl turned and glanced at him. He was quite different from the men she knew in the village, built with looser limbs, and with those fine, searching dark eyes of his, which seemed as though they would read down into her heart. She immediately associated him with some occult power, the same occult power which enabled Haidee to sit in her caravan and tell the future for village girls who sat dumbly before her, with jaws dropping.

She said : " I don't want to know my future."

" But everybody wants to know that," he said.

She shook her head. " I'm happy as I am;

why should I want to know about something which may be unhappy? I'd rather enjoy today."

It was a philosophy of life which he did not understand. For the first time in his life it struck him that the noise was raucous, and that he wanted to get away from it. The galloping horses still plunged up and down on their roundabout, with their fearsome painted nostrils and their yellow spots. He felt a longing to get away from the tune being droned, with the idiotic plaster figures in front aimlessly beating the air as though in some attempt at keeping rhythm. He wanted to escape.

He said: " Let's get away from here. I want to talk to you."

" Why should you want to talk to me?" she asked.

" I don't know. Why does a man want to talk to a girl ever? This is all noisy. You are not the kind of girl who ought to be with noise. Let's go into the field."

He indicated the field at the edge of the crowd, with the hedges rippling with the first light green and the primroses in the wet banks beneath them.

She still stared at him. He, for his part, knew that he fascinated her; he knew quite well that she liked him and that she wanted to talk with him, and realizing his power over her he gripped her wrist. "Come," he said.

IV

Shower down thy love, O burning light!
For one night, or the other night
Will come the Gardener in White,
And gathered flowers are dead, Yasmin.
JAMES ELROY FLECKER.

THEY went into the field, creeping through the hole in the hedge, where the brambles were budded, and the wild roses already showed the first green glimpses of awakening to the new year.

The girl followed Noah calmly now, making no sound, and he had hold of her hand to draw her through the hedge, and knew that the very feel of her made him throb, and gave him a curious delight that he had never experienced before.

It was wet under the hedge, with the sopping moisture of late spring, when the mists lie and the rains bring on the flowers. But out in the meadow itself, where the sun had warmed it, the grass was fine and dry, and there were daisies growing, and little ant hills with the earth crumbling in them.

"We can sit here," he said, and took off his coat for her to sit on. It was a fine warm coat, for he had money to buy good things, and the shirt under it was clean, for Haidee was scrupulous. The gipsies need never be confused with the tinkers, who are a happy-go-lucky race and do not care much what they wear, or how soiled it may be. He knew that she appraised the cleanliness of the shirt and that it surprised her.

"You're gipsy, aren't you?" she asked.

"Yes. My mother is the queen and I am her youngest son. I have two brothers and two sisters."

She said, "Aren't you ashamed of being a gipsy?" and her voice sounded tense, as though really she meant it. It was amusing to him.

"Ashamed? Why should I be? Why is one ashamed of being the son of a queen?"

"But of the gipsies?"

He shook his head. "You talk queerly. You don't know the real gipsies."

"They steal," she said.

"Not the real gipsies."

"They are dirty folk—my mother told me that; and whenever they come into the neighbourhood we miss things. Hens and things."

Again he laughed.

"You are thinking of the tinkers! They are

the scum of the earth. They are light-fingered and all property is their property. They don't care. The gipsies are not made that way; they have different ideas."

She sat there dubiously. He knew that she was weighing up facts, whether she ought to believe him against everything that she had ever been taught, or whether she ought to distrust him. She said nothing. He liked the brown rough skirt that she wore, and the silly thin stockings, and the little shoes which would never last for a couple of miles on a hard road. He liked the mauve jumper which clung revealingly to her figure, clinging to the slightness of her waist and the curve of her breasts.

He said: "You have been told that gipsies are wild and wicked—that is not true. Do I seem wild and wicked to you?"

"No," she said.

But he knew that she was amazed to find herself sitting here, with the daisies, and the little ant hills, and the man beside her.

"You live here?" he asked.

"My father works for the farmer on the hill. We live in that white cottage in the valley." She turned and pointed it out to him. It stood away from the other cottages and he saw that it had a roof which dipped, and that the sun slanted on

to the small lattice windows. A couple of fan-
tail pigeons strutted the thatched gable. He
had always thought that if ever he came to sleep
under a roof he would keep pigeons; the idea
appealed to him.

"You are happy there?" he asked.

"Very happy."

She was so much quieter than the gipsy girls
that he knew. About them there was a certain
flamboyance, an excitability which was arresting.
Save, of course, Roma, who was sulky, and who
sat away from the others, biting her fingers and
staring at them with those glowering dark eyes
of hers. Old Haidee said that her mother had
been frightened when the girl was coming, and
that it had affected the baby and she would always be that way.

This girl was not sulky like Roma, neither was
she flamboyant like the other girls. She sat
there smiling a little, as though she enjoyed the
quiet of the meadow, and the fact that the barking music of the roundabouts and the cries of
the men who ran the cocoanut shies had died
down into the distance.

"What is your name?" he asked.

"It is Fay—short for Frances, you know. Fay
Denvers."

"Fay means a fairy."

She laughed a little. "Yes, but there are no such things."

"No such things as fairies?" He laughed also. "But of course there are fairies; we believe in them. They are little folk who won't hurt you as long as you leave them well alone, but they turn spiteful if you anger them."

"That's nonsense."

He took her hand; there was nothing romantic about the touch, only the grip of a friend. "You believe in things in which I don't believe. I believe in things which you think are silly. Yet maybe we both are right."

"That's true."

"Your people don't like the gipsies?"

She didn't lie.

"No," she said.

"You think we are funny folk, but we are no funnier than some of your people. We believe that it is not right to sleep beneath a roof; we believe that a gipsy may read in the sky of what is coming to the world. No, not only the weather—that's easy! It's up there on the face of the sky for everybody to read."

"I can't read it."

"No, of course, but I can."

Eagerly she caught at his sleeve, and plucking the material was surprised to find that it was so good, and so warm. "What does it say now? I'll be able to prove if you are right. Tell me what the weather will be?"

He turned his face to the sky, pale hedge-sparrow blue, and flecked here and there with a cirrus of cloud, little white puffs shaped like smoke bursts from a gun, round, and circling away into the distance.

He wetted his finger and held it up to the wind. "Yes," he told her, "at sundown the rain will come, and it will rain all night. Colder to-morrow, you'll find, treacherous weather, with a dark sky, no more fine until the end of the week. We've been lucky to have a good day for the fair."

"I shall hold you to that," she said.

"You'll find it's right! You learn of the things inside houses, but we learn of the things outside. Don't you ever feel closed in, shut away, prisoned by the houses in which you live? Don't you ever feel that you want something more? To know where the road winds, and when the seas come, and what lies over the seas?"

"You don't go overseas?" she asked.

He laughed at that, and because now his tongue was loosened, he started telling her the story of what he had done with his life. The vans had rolled across the face of Europe in their

time, and they had come back here because
Europe was restless, and there was always
trouble, and Haidee said that the gipsy folk were
better here in England, where they could go on
their way unmolested.

He told her of Leipzig Fair, of the gayness of
Denmark and how once his mother had told
fortunes in the Tivoli gardens there, where all
Copenhagen goes crazy on a summer's night, and
staid old gentlemen burst balloons with pretty
singing girls, and throw roses at them, and are
severely shocked next morning when they think
of their nocturnal adventures.

He told her of Paris, and of Seville, city of all
gipsies, where they come from all countries, and
meet together, and talk together, and hold par-
liament outside the city.

As she listened, her pale blue eyes began to
glow like jewels. About her there was an
awakening interest, a stirring as though she
could not believe all that he said. He was a story
book to her, and to him she was a princess. She
was the Lorelei that he had dreamt about that
time when he had come along the road beside
the Rhine, with the caravans in a raggle-taggle
line behind his mother's. She was the princess
in the French castle high above the Seine, who is
supposed to look down with eyes like blue glass,

and sing a blessing on the sailors. She was the blue Madonna of Marseilles who prays for sailors.

He crossed himself.

She said: "Why do you do that? I did not think that you believed in God?"

"Not believe in God?" He stared at her in amazement, then leaned closer. "Who do you suppose made all this? The field, the daisies, even the little ants in that ant hill? Who do you suppose made the birds to fly, and the clouds for them to fly to, and the hedges for them to nest in? Who do you suppose made all these things?"

"Why, of course, God," she replied; "only I was told that gipsies were heathens."

"We are Catholics," he replied, "good Catholics"; and he drew out of the pocket of his shirt a small rosary, old and brown with beads like berries. Years ago, when he was a little child and had wandered along the face of a mountain in Austria, an old monk had given it to him. "With my blessing," the old monk had said, and together he and the boy had knelt before a wayside Calvary and had prayed to the God who made mountains, and edelweiss for the gathering, and the larks to sing to the new day.

She said: "I too am Catholic."

Instantly he knew that it was a bond.

" We cannot part now," he told her; " we must meet again. Tonight? When everybody is busy with the fair?"

" You say that it will be wet tonight?"

" Even so we can meet? Is there not some shelter?"

She thought for a moment, then she said: " There is a barn down by the river, an old wooden barn where the farmers store their hay. It is warm there and quiet. Nobody ever goes there. But my mother would be angry. She has warned me never to speak to gipsies."

" Will she know?"

His eyes challenged hers, and the blue eyes like glass dropped before the gaze. She said: " No, she won't know"; but he realized that it made her anxious to think that, probably for the first time in her life, she was going against her mother.

" Listen," he said, and held tight on to her wrist. " Listen, my child, my mother too would be angry, because she does not like such things. But we grow from boys and girls to men and women, and the time comes when we have to choose for ourselves, and choose rightly or wrongly. I choose to meet you tonight. You choose to meet me. Is that not so?"

" It is," she told him.

They went back to the fair, and as they crossed
the meadow with the daisies and the little dry
ant hills and the wet ditch where the primroses
were lifting small jaundiced faces, they held
hands.

V

For yesterday is but a dream
And tomorrow is only a vision,
But today well lived makes
Every yesterday a dream of happiness,
And every tomorrow a vision of hope.
From the Sanskrit.

THE rain came in the early evening. The sun
hid his face behind the dark dun clouds rolling
up against the wind. The blue died, and the
white clouds like puffs of smoke from some un-
seen gun trailed away. The rain began lightly,
with the promise of increasing in violence.
Haidee in her van stared out at it, cursing. It
meant that the villagers would gradually disap-
pear to their own homes; that the work of the
day was over, and there would be no further en-
joyment and money-making tonight. It had
been a good day and she had done well, but at
the same time she had hoped to do better.

It might mean that instead of making it a one-
day fair, they would stay on and reopen on the

morrow, which would mean a second day and night there.

Yes, she decided, that would be the thing to do. She gave up all idea of further fortune telling, unclipped the smooth corals in their brave brass settings, in which she had been married, and she set to work to get some supper.

They crouched under a dingy bivouac, with the rain increasing all the time, and a cold wind blowing across the fair field.

"Where's Noah?" she asked at last.

Nobody had seen him.

Noah, said Zilla, had been absent most of the day and had done badly by the hoop-la. She herself had had a depressing day because a crack shot had come to the rifle range and had insisted that the foresights had been filed down. This he had unfortunately proved, and had declared that unless it was made worth his while he would fetch the village policeman. The policeman was a dignified object with heavily waxed moustaches but very little intelligence. The gipsies knew this, but he represented the arm of the law, and as they were always up against the arm of the law, which had never been predisposed in their favour, they had no wish to start an argument.

Zilla had expressed surprise, and had declared that she could not think who had tampered with the rifle. She had given the man a handsome prize, the best they had, because it was the only means she could think of to keep him quiet. He had not kept quiet, but had been a nuisance to her most of the day, and the takings had fallen off considerably because he had told all his cronies about the rifle.

Zilla considered this was mean. He had done well out of it, and the filing of foresights was legitimate, in that it merely represented good business from her point of view. She was very angry. When the argument had been at its highest, she had looked round for one of her brothers to come to her aid. Noah had a suave tongue and was usually good in disposing of difficult situations, and he had been missing.

"All day," she told her mother, "never seen him, and the hoop-la's done badly enough."

"It was the rain."

Yet all the time Haidee knew, for her crystal had told her things only the other night. Dark it had been, as though raddled by storm. It had warned her that life would not be smooth and sunny, that there were tempests ahead in her own life, heavy ones.

"Let him be," she said, and stuck the clay pipe back in her mouth, hoping to gain some comfort from it, though her heart was restless.

She knew something was amiss. Just as she had always known. Just as she had always realized that he, the dearest of all her children, would one day pass through a valley of disquiet, and that she, watching him go through that valley, would herself be storm-tossed and bewildered.

They were standing on the threshold of that time. Here tonight at a fair with the ground sodden and the rain dripping down the gaudily painted posts of the swing boats and the shooting galleries. With the roundabouts wrapped in ground sheets and old sackings, and the dwarfs, who were to have given a show in their own little tent, sitting together in a bivouac eating cold sausages and drinking strong, bitter tea. She could see them from where she herself crouched.

It is tonight, she told herself.

Noah had gone down to the barn.

He had found no difficulty in locating it, because where all the other barns were built of brick with slated roofs, or were dutch barns made of tin and painted blue or red, this was very old. Its timbers were dark as the timbers of an aged ship, and it struck him as being very much like a ship in appearance, with its hulk lifted high against the sky. It stood on the edge of a deserted farmyard, far from the farm itself.

The yard was fenced round with iron fencing, and the gate, broken on its hinges, stood wide. Four farm carts were thrust into an open-sided shed, their shafts dipping forward, as though weary with the long day's work. In the walled-in inner yard pigs grunted and the smell of straw and leavings came to him and struck his nostrils not unpleasantly.

A horse chafed in its stable; he could hear the grate of a chain against a manger made of iron, and the chinking of its hoofs against the stone-cobbled flooring.

The barn was gloomy inside, but his eyes were used to darkness, for in the evening the gipsies did most of their hunting, and on dark nights they had to learn to see clearly.

He slipped in and saw that it was very high, and that one end was stacked with loose hay, from which came the essence of a long-spent summer. There were dead clovers and lucernes and sweet grasses all bundled together. A chaff cutter stood to one side, and he knew at the other end there had been corn, but that had nearly ended, and now there were but a few ears lying about and the faintly musty scent of harvest with it.

He sat down in the hay, comfortable, warm, and smelling pleasantly. He could hear the dripping of the rain on the roof; it was falling steadily, and he knew that the steadiness indicated that it had come to stay. It would rain all night, easing at dawn, but tomorrow would be stormy again, and there would never be a sign of blue in the sky.

He sat there chewing the long thin stems of grasses which were dried so that he could extract none of the sweet juices from them that he loved.

She will come soon, he told himself.

Then he saw the door open, and a chink of light appear, the grey light of the rain-sodden world. Fay slipped inside. He knew that she could not see, so sat very still. Her eyes would accustom themselves to the darkness, though it would take her some time; then she would see him.

At last he said, "I'm here," and saw that she jumped a little.

"I . . . I did not think that you would come in all this wet."

"What is the rain? It is nothing to me. It does not even come inside my clothes. I told you that it would rain, didn't I?"

"Yes, you did." She came nearer and sat down on the hay beside him. "My mother would be very angry if she knew of this. I don't know what she would say. It makes me afraid."

"When a girl grows up she must not be afraid. She has to choose for herself. She has to choose life."

"Yes, but this is so queer."

"Why is it queer? If I were one of the ploughboys of your village you would not think it queer?"

"No, of course not."

"Is it then because I am a gipsy?"

"I suppose so," she assented.

He said: "Let us forget. You and I are young. We have today. There is no yesterday, there never was, and there will be no tomorrow."

She ought to have been afraid, but she was not afraid; she let him take her into his arms and kiss her gently. They were not the wild demanding kisses of the village boys, who could be surprisingly insistent when it came to embraces; these were gentle caresses, and because of their gentleness they intrigued her even more.

She said: "You mustn't, honestly you mustn't; it isn't right."

"Do I frighten you?"

"No," she said truthfully, "no, you don't frighten me," and was amazed that she should turn and cling to him. Now he did not seem to be a stranger any more but somebody that she loved. She knew that her arms went round his neck, and that she let him kiss her, always respectfully, always gently.

He said: "I suppose I always knew that this would happen and I would love where I must not love."

"But we are young, we have our lives. You said we had to choose for ourselves."

"I know, but the gipsies are particular about marriages; they love only amongst their own tribe."

She had not thought of that. She had never supposed that the stooping to conquer could be from any but her own side. Her people considered themselves to be a great deal better than the gipsies, and she knew that her mother would have been horrified had she known of this meeting. She did not understand how Noah could tell her that his people would object, because she believed that the objections would be entirely one-sided.

"But they couldn't feel that way," she said.

"They could. They are a very proud people. Haidee is a queen."

"Is Haidee your mother?"

"Yes; she is wonderful."

"I wonder if I saw her? I and my sister went round the caravans."

"She tells fortunes."

"You don't mean the woman with the very bright eyes who was smoking a pipe?"

"Yes."

She said: "Oh, but to smoke a pipe! Surely you realize that is funny?"

"Your father smokes a pipe?"

"Yes, of course."

"Why not your mother if she likes it?"

"But she couldn't like it." She laughed a little. "How could she like it?"

"We don't see alike. That is the only trouble. Let us put aside the points that we don't understand, and stick to the ones that we do. You know that I love you?"

All her life she had wondered what she would say when she was challenged this way. Coyness, furtive glances, pretence; yet now none of those points availed. She had to speak the truth.

"Yes, I know," she said.

"What are we going to do?"

"I don't know," and still she clung to him.

He said: "It is raining so hard that probably the fair will go on tomorrow. If we lose a night, we try to make it up. There is tomorrow in which we can think and decide. Tomorrow we shall see the way out."

"There can't be a way out," she began.

"Why not?"

She turned in the dim light of the barn with the sweet scent of the hay and a forgotten summer about them. "You don't know my mother; you don't know my people; they'd have a fit!"

"Why any more than my people?"

"Well . . . you *are* gipsies."

"And proud of it."

There was something defiant about the ring of his voice and she noticed it; it was infectious. She realized that he spoke the truth, and that he believed that he had something to be proud about. There was that touch of royalty in his bearing, something she had read of in books which her mother would have hated to think that she was reading, but something which had made her understand him at this particular moment.

"I believe you," she said quite involuntarily.

"There must be a way out." His arms now had hold of her; not possessively, but gently, and there was about his wooing something very different from the roughness of the village men, something that she could appreciate.

"Please," she begged.

"I would not hurt you."

"I know that."

He said: "If there is a way out we will find it, and we will find it together."

After that they said no more, but sat there with thoughts too sweet to find expression in words, and with the delicate sound of the rain dripping from the old roof, like some stringed pizzicato music, striking a different note each time. The barn seemed to be full of memories, the memories of June days with the grass waist-high, and the moon daisies, and the sound of the haymaker going round the fields and taking its toll. So many dreams!

Much later he got up with his arm still round her, and they went out into the rain together. She drew her coat so that it formed a hood over her hair, and for a time they stood under the screening of the roof, with the drips falling just beyond them.

She said: "What do you do for a living? Surely you don't just run those cocoanut shies and things?"

"No. I make clothes pegs and rag mats and brushes in the winter, and sell them at cottage doors. I go hopping in the late summer, and we go to race courses all through the best months of the year."

She said: "Is there nothing else you can do?"

He did not know why the spirit suddenly moved him, for he said, "Yes, I can sing," and, standing there in the rain, lifted up his voice and

began one of the gipsy songs that his mother had
taught him when he was only a child on her knee.
The pure tenor voice rose and fell, caught the
echoes and set them reverberating with the
sweetness of the sound. Fay stood there amazed.
She had heard music as they heard it at home,
when Simon the cowman played his concertina
and they sang to it. There was the wireless too,
but somehow on that the voices always sounded
tinny and she did not like it. But this was music
of the kind that she had never heard before, the
clear, full-throated sound of the man who has a
natural gift for music, the kind of voice which
goes echoing through the Welsh valleys, round
the canals of Venice, and across the clear white
caps of the Alps.

" My goodness, you *can* sing!" she said.

VI

An airship slowly sailed, with whirring fans
A voyager in the new found realms of gold,
A shadowy silken chrysalis whence should break
What radiant wings in centuries to be.
                                        ALFRED NOYES.

SOMEBODY else heard the sound of the man's
tenor voice, rising and falling, as he passed
close to the barn.

Richard Heath was spending the inside of a

week with his brother, who was the vicar of the parish. Richard and his brother had very little in common save the bond which is of the family, and, blood being thicker than water, takes much to sever. Once a year Richard went through this annual penance and came to the vicarage sitting well back from the road and flanked heavily with laurels and evergreens, as though afraid that the common eye should peer in and desecrate the privacy.

There were ten years between Richard and Leonard Heath. Leonard had been idolized by his adoring mother, who had always maintained that he was such a good boy. He had been a little prig as a child, and had been well fitted for the college to which he was sent. Emerging, he had fulfilled all her dearest ambitions and had finally become a priest and had arrived here at this parish. He had married a worthy lady, with no bust and sparse hair, who followed the same evangelical trend of thought. He did not allow playing cards in the house, he maintained that brandy even in sickness was sinful, and he refused to permit his wife to knit on a Sunday even if it were for charity.

Richard, on the other hand, had none of Leonard's exquisite qualities; he was quite a bad lad. All the family finances having been expended on making Leonard what he was, Richard had had to put up with indifferent schooling, and finally, with no university to back him up, had at eighteen been more or less shovelled out into life to fend for himself.

Luck had done well by him.

He took a job in the office of a theatrical agent, made amiable friends, because he had one of those pleasant manners which attract people, and by the time that he was twenty-two he was part and parcel of a big combine. He had a genius for discovering talent. He worked for a Jewish firm, two large men, with even larger noses, but with kind hearts, which by the curious shape of their figures appeared to have sunk well down into their stomachs! But Richard knew them for what they were—kind, generous, and benevolent.

He was genuinely interested in the entertainment world. He went across to Bavaria and discovered a troupe of dancers there whom he brought back and starred in London. They were a great success. It was Richard who went to Castile and found the slim little bit of a girl with limpid eyes, and the gift of dancing that made even old Goldstein himself goggle and clap his hands. Richard could find talent where other people would pass it by. Who in the world would have located that girl in the dirty little Spanish tavern where she washed floors, or played at it, because washing was something they did not understand? Who but Richard would have found that cowherd in the Alps whose yodelling was so different from the others, like music, the fine cadence of a harp?

Richard crept upwards.

He became a partner with his firm, and he made a great deal of money. Surreptitiously Leonard and his wife saw pictures of the expensive flat that he occupied, with frescoes on the walls, and deep divans.

"It doesn't look nice to me," said Mildred, who always saw the worst in everything.

"It's Richard!" said Leonard with inference.

Yet he still came down to stay, and he was encouraged because his contributions to the offertory were very gratifying.

Richard had had a detestable couple of days, and was thanking Heaven that he would be getting back to London tomorrow. He had been to the fair in the hope of finding something there, but the gipsies were ordinary, and the usual fair girls a miscellaneous and not attractive selection. There was nothing that held his attention. Disappointedly he returned to the vicarage. The rain made it disheartening.

He found the meals unappetizing, because both Mildred and Leonard nursed a poverty complex with vigilance and refused to countenance any greater luxury than hash and rice pudding. This irritated Richard, because his father had left all he had to Leonard, as being the shining light of the family, and there was no need at all for this economy.

There was nothing to do in the vicarage, and, murmuring something about taking a walk, he came out.

Although it was raining, it was quite pleasant. The earth smelt sweetly, and there was the tinkle of raindrops in the naked branches of the trees, soughing a little together. As he walked, he heard the sound of a man singing. At first he could not believe his ears. He had had a miserable couple of days, and had hoped that the fair would provide something worth while; the fair proving to be abortive, he had resigned himself to his fate, and now, just as he had come to the conclusion that there was nothing to find here, he heard the man singing. It was an extraordinary compass.

He stood quite still to listen.

The voice had qualities usually denied to mankind; it had the trilling of the nightingale as a natural gift; it had the cadence of the lark.

Richard's expert ear recognized the fact that here was a compass which could be trained to do more. He turned sharply, and walked in the direction of the voice.

He came to the barn raising its dark timbers against the stormy wet sky. He saw the two standing there, the man's arm round the girl, and the girl drawing close to him. He had just stopped singing.

Richard came up to them.

"Was that your voice?" he asked.

"I was singing," said the man, and his speaking voice was soft and honeyed, so that instantly Richard knew that he was of one of the gipsy tribes.

"You know you have a marvellous voice?"

"No. I sing because I like singing."

Richard said: "I want to talk to you. I'm sorry to butt in like this, but a voice of the type that you have got is worth a great deal of money. Can't I talk to you?"

Then the girl spoke.

"I'd better be getting along," she said; and her voice was ordinary, the voice of any village girl, and not one of the tribes.

"You can't leave me like this," said Noah quickly. "When will I be seeing you again? When? Tomorrow morning, here?"

But she shook her head.

"What, with the whole village to see? I daren't. Think what mother would say."

"Then tomorrow night, here?" he asked.

"Very well." But Richard knew that her voice was vague, as if she were not sure of it.

He put in a spoke.

He said: "You may not realize it, but this man has a marvellous gift. He's going to be a great man. Did you know?"

Fay laughed nervously. She did not know what to make of it, and felt uneasy. Anyway, she would get into dreadful trouble at home if they knew that she was out here with one of the gipsies, even though the vicar's brother had come along, and said that Noah would be great. She had thought herself that his voice was lovely, but she had not thought that it was anything as lovely as all that.

She said, "I must be going," and turned away, digging her hands into the pockets of her coat, tramped off down the lane to the cottage where she lived. Neither of the men made the slightest movement to accompany her. Richard was glad to be rid of her, Noah could not understand why she had wanted to go so suddenly.

"Let's talk inside the barn," said Richard.

Noah followed him without a word.

They went into the dimness and sat down on the hay where half an hour ago he and Fay had sat, and had talked of the beautiful imaginings which love gives to people. To Noah, who was an idealist, the other conversation was something inescapable; and although he tried to focus on what this new friend was saying, his mind kept wandering back to the moments with Fay, her sweetness, the way her hair grew in little baby curls on her neck, and the pale blue loveliness of her eyes.

"Listen," said Richard, "what do you do with your life? What are you?"

"I'm with the gipsies. Haidee is my mother."

"She's their queen, isn't she?"

"Yes. There are five of us. I am the youngest."

"I see; and you do nothing in particular for a living?"

Almost mechanically his voice droned on. "I make pegs, and mats, and brushes in winter; we go to race courses, and to fairs, and hopping in the summer."

Richard said: "Have you never thought of singing? Singing for a living?"

"No."

For Noah had none of the avariciousness of the usual gipsy; he sang because he loved life, and because it was a gift which had been given to him which he did not want to harness. He had never thought of anything more.

"I sing when I am happy," he said, and it was the truth.

Richard said: "That girl who was with you just now—she isn't gipsy?"

"No, she lives in the village."

"Have you known her long?"

"Long enough to know how I feel," he answered with a little dry laugh.

Richard nodded. He said: "Her people would never let you marry her because they are the most rigid type. But they would let you marry her, and be only too glad, if you were a great singer. You know that, don't you?"

Slowly Noah turned his face to Richard's. His eyes could pierce the dimness of the barn so that he could recognize truth when he saw it.

"You mean that would make her marry me?"

"Of course. Here is your chance. You have got a marvellous natural voice; it needs training, it is true, but I'd take a chance on that. A year, a couple of years, and you'd be top of the bill." He was beginning to get excited with the idea, and to develop it. "You'd be a star bigger than any of the others that I have ever found, even that Spanish girl."

"What would I have to do?"

"You'd have to come to London and train. I know that sounds hard, but everybody who wants to be somebody and to get somewhere has to do something that they don't want to do really. You know that, don't you?"

"Yes," said Noah.

"I've got it in my power to make you what you want to be. I'll do it too."

"It would mean leaving Haidee?"

"Yes."

There was silence. Noah was going back to the time when she had told him of this. When she had looked into her crystal for herself and had seen in its dark ebb and flow some vision which flickered across her own life. She had sat there with her hand in his, and he had sensed some remote pain, some strange birth pang which came to her again and again with recurring force. He said: "I knew this would come. What do I do?"

Richard had learnt from experience that it was futile trying to force matters.

"Meet me here in another twenty-four hours," he said; "you'll have had a chance to talk it over with the girl then, with your mother, with your people. But let me tell you there is money in this. Real money. You know that, don't you? Everything that you can ever want."

"I don't want much," said Noah.

He had never thought beyond the hedgerows which bordered the roads in his life, nor higher than the trees which arched those roads like the lovely green transepts of some natural cathedral. He had not thought of anything save drifting through life as his people had always drifted, with good years, and bad years, and a stocking thrust into some safe corner of the van, and the knowledge that life always yielded something worth having.

He had not wanted money. But now, for the first time, he thought of a woman in his life, and he knew that women do want money, and they want a lot of it.

"I'll meet you here," he said, and got up.

"Goodnight," said Richard.

VII

Here is the mill with the humming of thunder,
Here is the weir with the wonder of foam,
Here is the sluice with the race running under
Marvellous places, though handy to home!
ROBERT LOUIS STEVENSON.

FAY went home slowly. She could not analyse her own feelings. What she had been doing had been against all the doctrines that she had been

taught as a child; she had always been told that
the gipsies were dirty, that they stole children,
and that they thieved. She did not know why
she had been attracted to Noah in the first place,
and it bewildered her to think that now she
wanted to see him again.

Fay was the second daughter of Daniel
Denvers, the shepherd. Her mother was a tried,
waspish little woman, with sandy hair scraped
back from a freckled face, and a body bent with
too frequent child-bearing and hands gnarled
from too persistent attention to the washtub.

Fay had been born in the white cottage with
its two rooms upstairs and the little corner room
which leaked with the rain; it had a front room
which they never used, and the back kitchen
where the whole family lived. That entailed
Mother and Father, with his boots smelling
of sheep dung, and his old coat, which smelt of
lambs. There was herself and her elder sister
Gladys, who was in service now and worked in
the next village. Gladys had been waspish like
her mother, and had been appointed Fay's
nurse. Fay had suffered badly at Gladys's sharp
hands, and knew her bitter tongue.

But when Gladys went into service, Fay had
been appointed nursemaid of the pack of children. The eldest, an obnoxious brother called

Bert, suffering from perennial catarrh, and who told his mother anything which he felt would benefit himself at all; Eileen, a fat child with adenoids, who nearly broke Fay's back every time she had to lift her, and Jimmy, who wasn't quite " the thing "; Mother had had a fright two months before he was born and it had affected the baby. The youngest was Doris, another fat, unlovely child, who cried a great deal, and had to be dragged about because the old pram had dropped to pieces in the effort of wheeling out the whole of this family.

Fay ever since she was nine had had to mind a baby. She had grown so tired of them, and so wearied with their infantile incontinencies, with their muling and puling, and insistent demands upon her time and attention, that sometimes she prayed she might never have children herself. It would not have been so bad if her mother had had some idea of management. But the waspish little Mrs. Denvers had no idea at all. Her cottage was scrupulously clean in that it reeked of Sunlight soap and carbolic. She mended their clothes assiduously, and she worked hard, but she took a pride in her efforts, and was for ever telling everybody that all this was her great merit.

She believed in smacking the young frequently and on any provocation. She did not do this spitefully, but because she believed that it was the thing to do. She had a set code by which she brought them up. It was the code of her grandmother.

Daniel himself was a big, dour man. He did not debate on family matters, but left the up-bringing of his children to his wife. He believed in church twice on Sunday, and in certain standards which were obviously those of Sunlight soap and carbolic and well-mended clothes. Twice a year he went out and got gloriously drunk, as an assertion of his own rights to his wife and family. Fair night was one of these occasions.

At all other times of the year he was abstemious, a fine shepherd, for ever tramping the hills, and attentive to the lambs. He lost less ewes for the farmer than any other shepherd for miles around, and was worth his money.

As she walked home through the rain Fay reflected upon these matters. She was eighteen. She had been into service for two years between sixteen and now, at a doctor's over the hill, and had recently left because she thought that she was worth more money, and the mistress would not give her a rise. Her mother had insisted that she must come home and look for another place; anyway, two years gave her a good reference, and she could do better for herself.

Unfortunately, Fay had not been home a fortnight before she caught measles from Jimmy
and Doris, which meant that she must delay
looking about her for a place.

During this time she had met James Day.

James Day was the miller from the mill at the
far end of the village, set straddling across the
water, with the big sluice gates, and the reeds
growing tall, and a single silver-green willow
tree beside it. James was in the thirties, so that
he seemed to be an immense age to Fay, who at
eighteen felt anything over twenty was old. He
was a fine-looking man with a florid face and
dark hair smarmed down. He was a good miller,
and well off, so the people in the village said, for
he owned his mill, and the great wheel which
turned, and the sluice gates, and the fields the
other side where he grew corn and barley.

"He's setting his cap at you, my gel," said her
mother when James came twice in one day to see
the family, whom hitherto he had almost ignored, "and you might do worse. He has got a
tidy sum set by, and his first wife left him a
packet, so they say."

Fay remembered the story of the first wife,
which had been one of the village sensations
when she was only a little scrap of a girl, and

before Jimmy and Doris were even born. The first wife had come from London, and was a stylish woman whom James had loved deeply. But she had been queer with it, and had had moods, and had, so the village declared, her ups and downs with the moon. This way and the other she had havered, nice when she was in the mood, but unaccountable at times, doing strange deeds and saying strange things.

Coming home from school the children would see her sitting on a pile of flints beside the road, with her shoes and stockings off, and staring at the sun, like a caged eagle in some zoo. They were all afraid of her.

Then she would be quite sensible, and would meet them and give them comfits from the village shop, and talk to them about fairies. But they suspected her, because they could not forget the woman who sat on the pile of flints at the roadside, with the little short July poppies growing about her, and staring at the sky as though it were a freedom beyond bars.

She became worse.

Then one night there was a scandal rushing through the village, so that they stood in little groups at their doorways and chattered together.

It seemed that she and James had had a quarrel, and he had locked her in her room because he knew that the moon was in the wrong phase and that she did not know what she was doing. She had resented this. It had been late September, with the river mist riding up, so that it was difficult to see everything that was happening. James had had to go into the village about some sacks of flour, and he went believing that she was all right, locked in the room from which she could not escape, and in which she could not harm herself.

But he was wrong.

The grocer came with his little travelling car, from which he sold tea and sugar and currants and plums. She opened the window and called down to him. "I've locked myself in," she told him, "and let the key drop and can't find it. Come up here and help me out."

The man who drove the van was new to the job; he did not know of her crazy mind, with its curious warp. He came up the stairs, and expressed surprise to find the key in the door, but he let her out. She came down the stairs, her eyes dancing. He said afterwards that he noticed something about her, curious and flittering, as though she were not a real person, but some butterfly which stopped to singe its wings at a candle for a moment.

Then he had to get on with his rounds.

Nobody knew what came to the poor creature then, but when James got home from barter with his sacks of flour he found her swinging from the silver-green willow tree, with a noose around her neck, and her body no longer a body, but a mere helpless shadowy form, which swung like a leaf.

For some time he did not come out of the mill, they all thought that he would be a recluse, and never smile again. He seemed to have no use for the world. The children, who in summer had been in the habit of taking a swing up to the willow tree, and swinging there, gave up the idea. The story that a ghost swung there on an autumn night ran like a forest fire through the village, and left behind it a black trail.

To this very day no children ever swung on the silver-green willow tree, even though a generation had grown up, and Violet Day's grave in the churchyard was old, and sunk in, and the violets which somebody had set to grow there had straggled right over it, and smelt of earth, and loveliness, and hope, in the first days of March.

James Day had grown quieter.

He went about his work, and he never mentioned the wife who had died there. A woman from the village came and did for him, and did well, but she said that he seldom spoke to her. He seemed to have lost all interest in life outside his mill, and he did not encourage visitors.

But Mrs. Denvers had noticed the way that he had come twice to the cottage to see Fay; she had noticed the way that he looked at her. She was a shrewd woman, and quick to make a good bargain.

"You'd be doing well for yourself, gel," she said.

Fay liked James, but nothing more. She cared deeply already for Noah. Walking home through the rain, she knew that she had no right to care, because her mother would fly into one of her rages if she once learnt that Fay had been with him. It was something that she could not hope to live down. But, she told herself, they would not know.

She went round to the back of the house, by the butt where the water dripped from the roof and so gave her mother soft water for washing the clothes. She opened the door.

The lamp was lit already, and they were sitting round it. Her mother with her eternal stockings to darn, her father with the Sunday newspaper which he made last him all the week, and Jimmy, and Doris, and Eileen, huddled on to the old sofa they had bought at a rummage sale four years ago, and which was an extra bed, or form, or whatever they liked to make of it. Only Bert was away. These days he had a girl over at another village. His mother did not know and thought that he was at the vicar's night class, and was therefore satisfied. But Fay did know and she realized how furious her mother would be if it ever came out.

"So you've come back," said her mother, and rose.

Instantly Fay realized that she knew! She could see it in the dilated eyes, and the small dry mouth, with the missing front tooth through which the small tongue darted repeatedly like a snake's tongue. Somebody must have seen her, and had taken the tale home as a joke. It was just the sort of thing for ever happening in the village.

"Yes, I've come back," she said.

The three children on the sofa stared at her; they had obviously been listening to the story churned out by her mother, much like the tune on the roundabouts at the fair. Her father put down his paper.

"Where've you been?" he asked.

"Up the village."

"Who've you been along?"

"Why?" she asked.

Her mother rose. She had been bottling up all her energies for this moment. As she got up the stockings that she had been darning fell in all directions, the rolled-up ones shooting out like cannon balls.

She said: "You think we don't know. You think we haven't heard; well, we have. You've been along of the gipsies. You, my own daughter, a clean-living, decent girl, along of one of them gipsy lads."

"I met one of them. There was nothing in it. We talked."

"You talked to a gipsy. You who call yourself my daughter. Don't you know what the gipsies are? A dirty, lying, thieving lot. And you dare stand there and not be ashamed to own up to me that you've been along of them."

"There was nothing to be ashamed of," she said.

Her father turned then.

"Nothing to be ashamed of? You, a decent girl, out with the gipsies! Everybody knows what they are."

She remembered Noah with his gentle voice, and the quiet way that he had stroked her hand, his protestations about the gipsies, and she knew that whereas at the time she had not been sure, now she was quite sure. He had been right. His people had a dignity that her people had not got, even if they were God-fearing, even if they were respectable. She preferred Noah with his quietness to the continual storm which thrust its way through this cottage home of hers.

" If you weren't the age you are, I'd tell your father to take his belt to you," said her mother. " Be off to your room, and don't you let me see your face again. And if you dare go near them gipsies any more, I'll give you what you deserve, age or no age, and that's flat."

Fay stood her ground.

" I'm eighteen," she said; " I could go right away today and you couldn't make me come back. That's the law."

"And where do you think you'd get meat and drink?" asked her father.

" And where do you think you'd get a good bed to lie in?" snapped her mother. "And a mother and father to love you and care for you and bring you up proper? Somebody's been putting ideas in your head, silly ideas, and a long way they won't get you, I don't think. Standing up to me, you impudent little baggage."

She appealed to her father.

She might have known the futility of that, for long ago he had been worn down by the snappings and railings of his wife. Long ago he had learnt of the hopelessness of attempting to stop her talking.

Fay had the horrible feeling that the three children sat staring at her from the old sofa, three goggle faces, with no sense in them, particularly poor little Jimmy, who wasn't "the thing." They stared at the row; all they hoped was that it would not come their way, for they were used to slappings and pinchings, and the lashings of hard words. They had a respect for their father's belt.

"Don't you talk to me," said her mother.

"I don't see why I should be treated like this. I've done nothing."

"Nothing or not, you aren't doing that sort of thing here. I've a mind to turn you out. Where would you go, do you think?"

Fay cowered before that thought. When she had said that she would go, she had not thought out the problem. She was a simple-minded girl who had been brought up here and who had no idea of how she would fare outside the village. She became acutely conscious of the fact that the world is a large place, and that it is not kind to waifs. She had no money. The little she had saved from her wages had been taken from her for her keep by her mother. She had a few clothes, the prints, and the one black afternoon frock, a handful of aprons which she had collected, very little else.

Although she was agitating for a place to the schoolmaster's wife in a little town ten miles away, nothing had materialized yet. She could not go tonight, as she would have liked to do. If Noah had been of different birth maybe she could have run to his people—she had heard of that kind of thing happening before—but Noah had inferred that his people would not be pleased and the idea horrified her.

She turned sullenly and went up to bed. She heard her mother screaming something after her in that raucous voice. She knew that she was hungry, she had had no supper, and now would not get any; what was more, she dare not go down again to ask for it. She sank down on the mattress which she had shared for years with Gladys, but now used with Eileen and Doris. It was clean, but very hard.

She sat there miserably.

She felt that she was too old for this kind of punishment and that her whole soul rebelled, but that there was nothing she could do.

Then across the valley she heard the sound of a voice singing, and she knew that it was Noah as he went back to his caravan. He sang like the nightingale—she did not know when she had ever heard such trills, such crescendoes, such decrescendoes—and she knew that he sang because he was happy. He did not know that some busybody had already been chattering about her.

How would she get out to see him the next night? she asked herself; how would she get away to him? Because she had got to see him again. He could not go out of her life for ever at this particular moment.

VIII

Dead dreams of days forsaken,
Blind buds that snows have shaken,
Wild leaves that winds have taken,
    Red strays of ruined Springs.
             SWINBURNE.

NOAH walked singing towards the vans, clustered together in the corner of the field close to the blind hedge.

Tonight fame had dazzled across his path. He did not know when he had felt so ecstatic about things, nor so confident. In the afternoon he had thought how hopeless was the situation. Fay attracted him. She attracted him by contrast—the blueness of her eyes, the gold softness of her hair, the paleness of her skin. He had seen other gipsy men attracted by just such beauty, and knew how Haidee had reacted to it. Himself also. He himself had felt that they betrayed the tribes when they married yellow-haired country girls, who bore them yellow-haired children.

He knew also how Haidee would take such a suggestion. "You'll hurt me more than any of the others have been able to hurt me, because I love you more," she had said.

Then he had thought that it was so much nonsense, something from which he could escape, which was quite matterless. Now suddenly he knew that this was the way that he would hurt her, and it would go deep.

But now suddenly, because he was so much in love, he was not feeling the same way about Haidee. The swift infatuation had taken the place of the tender, deep love for his mother. He had changed. He had crossed the Rubicon which lies between boyhood and manhood, and with it he had said goodbye to those fond em-braces, the climbing on to her knee, and fond-ling her swarthy cheek with his little fat hands. Never more would he go to her for consolation and for help in the difficulties which beset him. He knew that now. He was a man, he thought as a man, and he lived as a man, and a man needs a woman to bear him company.

It is never his mother who walks beside him, but his love; and who better than his first love?

He came to the vans drawn under the hedge in the corner of the field, and he saw the lights in them, like a cluster of small stars. He would have crept into the hammock spread beneath his mother's van, along with the lurchers tied there. and watching him with wideawake eyes and lolling tongues, because he did not want to disturb her. He was in no mood for argument, nor for lying, and he felt that this was not the hour in which to face the truth.

She must have been watching for him.

The top half of the van door opened, and he saw her framed in the square of light. She had taken off her corals and her best lace, but there were gold rings in her ears, and her dark hair was drawn back from her brow, and coiled in a curl like a rope on the nape of her neck. He thought that he had never seen so much majesty about her, so much dignity, as at this moment, when she leaned out of the van into the rain with the gold rings in her ears, and her eyes like black glass beads.

"Noah?"

He said: "Yes, I'm here."

Below the van the lurchers watched him; in the dim shadow their eyes were eerily luminous. They made no sound, for they were well trained. Above, her eyes watched him and they were eyes like stars.

"Are you coming here?"

"Very well."

He went slowly up the steps that he himself had made last winter, firm, strong steps made of good boarding, and they would last many a year. He opened the door into the van itself, small, and full of fetid air, for the lamp was burning and everything was closed. On the stove a kettle boiled; he could see the marks on the shining steel where it must have boiled over. He knew that must have made her mad, and could not think how it was she had allowed it to happen.

Then he saw.

She had been reading her crystal, for the thing was on the side, just as she had left it to come to him on the first sound. Smooth and round it glowed, as though it were filled with cloudy water.

He sat down opposite to her.

She said: "I know where you've been."

"Then why did you call me up here?"

"I wanted to talk." He knew her so well that

he realized that she was highly emotional. Her
furtive eyes watched him, and her hands, usually
so still, plucked at the corner of the gaudy scarf
that she wore twisted round her throat.

He noticed it all.

" It's getting late."

" But not so late. There'll be supper soon,"
and she nodded in the direction of the steel
stove where there was a saucepan cooking.

" I'm not hungry."

She said: " Why don't you tell me about
her?"

" Her?"

" Yes, the girl! I saw it in the crystal. I
knew this would come; it was written there. I
know it'll pass too. That is what you don't
know."

" I love her," he said, and the words sounded
crude, but he could think of nothing else. He
did love her.

She sat down heavily and began to nod, her
hands folded on her high stomach, and those
fingers still plucking at the multicoloured fringe
of the scarf.

He said: " It's no good. The time has come
when I'm a man and I go my own way."

" I am still your mother," she answered.

" I know that, but even being my mother does

not give you the right to twist my life as you want it." And then, as if it worried him: "What did you see in your crystal?"

"There was a girl. She had yellow hair and blue eyes, and another man wanted her."

That was news to him, but he gave no sign that he did not know it.

"Go on," was all that he said.

"The other man will get her. He has a big house and fine money, and land. He had another wife, but she hanged herself on a willow tree outside the house. I know, because I can see it in my crystal."

"I don't believe in crystals."

She said nothing, only watched him with those sharp eyes of hers that saw everything.

"What else did you see?" he asked after a minute.

"The man—who was the man you met to-night who offered you riches?"

"He came up to me in the lane. He is the brother of the parson here, so she told me, and he has something to do with people who sing. He wants me to go to London, to train me to sing."

She made a face at that.

"You to go to London? A gipsy who has never slept under a roof, and does not know

what it feels like to have a bed. You can't do
that."

"I don't see why not."

"Listen," she said—and now she was very
much in earnest, leaning forward in her chair
and watching him with those indignant eyes of
hers—"listen, you are standing at a crossroads,
and there are two ways that you can take. The
way to happiness, the way that you will have to
take in the end, is here in this van beside me,
with a kingdom to follow, and the subjects of
the tribe. When I die, you will be king, you
know. You are my favourite son."

He said nothing.

"This is here for the asking. This is your
world. It is the world which for a time you will
turn your back upon."

"What shall I do?"

"The crystal tells me that you will go out of
this world and follow fame. You will become
great. But fame will not bring you what you
seek, for you will not marry your yellow-haired
girl; she will be unfaithful to you."

"That isn't true."

Even as his mother spoke he felt that this was
jealousy, and he suspected her of inventing it
to make her case stronger. Not that he had
known her cheat him ever in the years when

they had been together. But this moment, this particular moment, he was dubious of her, because love is a jealous emotion, in particular the kind of love which he felt for Fay.

"It is true," she said, "and you will find the truth of it, and come back here so many years ahead. You will find that she has cheated you, and you will turn from her here to this very spot where the vans will be drawn close to the hedge; just as today. I may not be here, but you will come back here, as a king to his own."

"It's nonsense!" he said.

She did not deny him. She went to the stove and taking the lid off the saucepan peered down at the contents. He could see the outline of her profile against it, and noted how young she looked for her years, and about her that careless grace which is entirely gipsy. She walked as all women walk who have gone barefoot across the world, and whose bodies are poised, and who carry themselves with a simple dignity.

"Need this thing come between us?" he asked.

She said: "I have turned away from the tribe others who have tried to marry golden-haired girls who sleep under a roof: how can I make a difference for my own son?"

"But you will?"

She shook her head.

"I know the laws, and to the laws I keep," she said doggedly.

"Then I shall go to London and learn to sing, and make much money," he answered, and for the first time he felt exhilarated in that he knew this chance was being given to him by the strange man they had met tonight.

She said: "Yes, you will go to London and learn to sing, and make much money, but that is no cure for a broken heart, and you will learn that too."

Methodically she went on arranging the supper, pouring the rabbit out on to a plate for him, but he turned from it.

"I'm not hungry," he said.

He got up and went down the little wooden steps which he himself had made only last winter. She never made a sound. He knew then that she meant what she said and that she would not try to detain him. She would let him go, even if it broke her own heart, because that was the law of the tribe, and she was queen of the tribe, and had to set an example to the others. He went below to the hammock and, creeping through the wet grass to it, slung there.

He knew that he would not sleep.

IX

Follow a shadow,
    it still flies you;
Seem to fly it,
    it will pursue.
               BEN JONSON.

YET Noah slept until the dawn, which rose early, a creature of pearl. The other men were already up and about, and the lurchers were across the field, because on their hunt the food of the day depended. The dawn touched the gaudy painting of the shies and the ill-cloaked roundabout with crude fingers which showed it up in an unlovely light. Even Noah noticed it.

As a child he had believed the roundabout to be one of the most beautiful things that he had ever seen. He had stood dumbly as a little boy before its ornamental façade, with the stupid little plaster figures jerking out their wooden accompaniment, and the gaudy horses rising and falling, with their imitation snorting nostrils, and their fierce eyes staring blankly at the onlookers.

They are fine horses, he had thought, and had thrilled, and had thought covetously of the day when he was a man; he would save up his money and possess horses fine as these, and great gold-painted organ tubes, and music which made everybody turn to stare.

But as he grew older he had become tired of the bright colours. He wondered if he were truly gipsy, and once had stopped to look at his hands, and his swarthy cheeks and the dark hair which curled and nothing would make it lie flat. He had known that he was all gipsy. But perhaps it was that a second being stirred within him, the artist who loved song. And the artist who loved song saw that the roundabout was tawdry, that the cocoanut shies were cheap and shoddy with their chipping paint and their tired awnings. Even the smart new vans, freshly painted, with their vigorous yellow wheels and the decorated scarlet hubs, even those were inartistic.

He could see it; and he was a gipsy!

This morning he saw it more than ever. A trembling dawn, with streaks of fire shot through its tissue, promising a wet spell before the night. But the dawn was of beauty; its red was not sullen, nor too gay, its orange was a living fire, not paint splashed on, out of a cheap pot. It had fineness, and tenderness, and was beautiful.

It showed up the crudity of the fair field badly. He saw the thorn hedge alongside where he lay, and the earth ditch with the primrose, and here was the same exquisite fashioning of the dawn.

He got up.

He washed himself carefully, and went across the field with his hands dug in his pockets and a muffler round his throat. The others did not notice him, but he had an idea that, from her van, his mother was watching. Her bright eyes missed so little.

He went into the village, and up the street, where the women were washing steps, and drew away from him as he passed, because they felt that he was unclean. He was used to that. They had strange superstitions these women; they believed still that gipsies stole children—as though they had not enough of their own without wanting others. Why, Zilla had not been married five years and had two chubby boys, and another before Whitsuntide. They had prolific families.

He came to the vicarage at the top of the hill, away from the rest of the village, as though it felt itself in some degree superior and wished to be aloof.

He turned in at the gate.

He noticed the shrubberies, and the lawn beyond, and the wide border where there were daffodils and narcissus growing, and the elm tree just bursting into leaf. A robin perked inquisitively on the arm of a garden seat which, by its colour, must have been left out all the winter.

He wondered that the tinkers had not had it!

He could hear the sounds of cocks crowing in a pen round to the back of the house, and wondered about them. There sounded to be a good penful, and he knew that gentlemen usually kept a goodly stock. A hen was pleasant for the stew pot; sometimes they were lucky in getting them. He marched on.

The drive curled round into a wide expanse where you could turn a car. A monkey tree grew towards the end of it, and an apple tree, which soon would be pearly with blossom. A terrier ran out and sniffed at his heels, but, evidently deciding that he was a friend, wagged his tail pleasantly, and went off again to his place on the oakum mat.

Noah went round to the back of the house, where a tall pump stood sentinel over the flagged back yard, and where there came the scent of wallflowers planted in a border under the study window. He knocked sharply.

The maid who came in answer looked surprised to see him, if not a little afraid.

She pulled herself together.

"It's no good your coming begging here," she said, but her voice trembled, and he knew that she was alarmed.

"I'm not begging. I saw the vicar's brother last night. Mr. Richard is his name. I wanted to see him again."

"I wonder if that's true?" said the girl, now very dubious indeed.

"It's true enough. You go and ask him."

She said: "Very well. You wait here"; and she shut the door upon him and shot the bolt, as though she doubted the goodness of his purpose.

He smiled to himself.

After a little while he heard her footsteps coming echoing down the flagged passage, and the bolt was unshot, and the door opened again. She looked rather cross.

"The vicar says as how Mr. Richard is walking in the orchard, and if you go down there you'll find him. Catch his death, he will, one of these days."

"Which way is the orchard?"

"Down there," she said, and pointed to a small red gate at the farther end of the yard.

He followed the direction she had indicated. The gate opened on to a shrubbery of elder and euonymus, and round by a rock garden to the steep of a garden laid out primly with flower beds, and descending into an orchard where the grass grew coarse and long, and where the apple trees touched one another. He saw now that the hen pens were to the left, wired in, and a padlock on the door, which bore out that which he had already suspected, in that he thought the tinkers were likely to come trespassing here.

They were white fowls, with scarlet combs and giblets, and he knew by the look of them that they laid well, and made good birds for eating.

He walked on, down the garden to the grass of the orchard, and he saw at the other end Mr. Richard walking, wearing a leather short jacket, and a big green muffler round his throat and his head bare to the wind. He looked a fine man, Noah considered, and he was attracted to him.

He went through the grass, lifting his feet as only gipsies can, with his body straight and upright, and never sign of age in his flexible limbs.

Richard saw him.

"Why, hello, if it isn't the singer," he said. "Now, what news have you brought me?"

"I have come to know what you can do for me?"

Richard nodded.

"I am prepared to take you to London. To

train you, and make you a first-class singer.
There is no doubt about it. You'll get there.
Haven't you ever wanted to see your name in
electric lights on Shaftesbury Avenue? Well,
you *will* see it."

"It'll take long?"

"Not very long."

Then suddenly Noah opened his heart.

He told Richard of his mother, who was a
queen, and who would turn him out because he
was in love with a girl who had yellow hair.
She had turned out other members of the tribe
for the same thing, and she would never spare
her own son. He wanted to make her eat her
words.

He told him of the girl whom he had met so
suddenly, and had been so amazed at the over-
whelming passion which had suddenly risen
within him. Just at first it had been only attraction, but in the barn last night it had deepened
to something more. He had no position in the
world; the thought of marriage was entrancing
but impossible. Her people were as sternly
against it as were his people, and unless he could
strike out on his own and get money he could
not marry her.

Richard listened to it.

He said: "See her again. Tell her that next

time the fair comes to the meadow you will come back to marry her. Ask her to stay true to you for one whole year, and you will come back to claim her."

A year seemed interminable to Noah. He said so. Another summer, trailing away into the hop season, and the October, and the time when the vans were stacked by and he made pegs and mats, ready for the new spring. But Richard laughed at that. This year he would not be hopping, neither would he be making rag mats and cheap clothes pegs to barter from door to door. He would be building up a career, note by note, and he would burst out as a new star in the firmament of the entertainment world.

Noah said that he was ready.

To him the entertainment world was something quite away and vain. He knew the dwarfs who had their show on every fair ground, and the fat lady who was to be seen at bigger fairs, and the girl who could lift a horse with her teeth, and do feats of great strength. Sometimes when he grew tired of the hoop-las he would peep through the tents and see these entertainments, lit by flares, with the crowd jostling together, and the show on some cheap little stage.

"It will not be like that," said Richard slowly.

How would he live? Noah asked, because he would have to live during this training time; a man could not feed on air.

Richard understood that.

He had had to put money behind the Spanish girl whom he had brought all the way from Castile. If a man or a girl were to be a draw, they were worth backing. A couple of pounds a week would keep a man like Noah very comfortably in some back street of London.

" I will see to that," he said, and gave him a card. " This is where you come to see me."

On the card was written:

THEATRE ROYAL,
SHAFTESBURY AVENUE.

He read it, and nodded.

" Yes, I'll do it."

" And mind you tell that girl you'll be back in a year's time."

" You're sure it is true?"

" Quite sure," said Richard and laughed. He had never been surer of anything.

X

Out of the mid-wood's twilight
Into the meadow's dawn,
Ivory-limbed and brown-eyed
Flashes my Fawn.
O Hunter, snare me his shadow!
O nightingale catch me his strain!
Else moo struck with music and madness
I track him in vain!

OSCAR WILDE.

FAY was having a very difficult time at home. She had got up early, for there were the children to prepare for school, and her mother had been up betimes getting her father his breakfast, and his dinner tied into his handkerchief, and to start him on the day. He was always away by dawn at this time of the year, and sometimes did not come back all night, because the ewes were lambing, and he was often wanted in the yard with them.

The children were lazy, and had to be hurried and chivied. She helped her mother with their breakfast and started them on the road. Long before that her mother had begun her raillery.

"A fine thing it was last night. You out there with one of them gipsies, and the whole place talking. It's into trouble you'll be before we know where we are."

Fay held her tongue.

"So it's sullen you are playing at?" Her mother could never let a thing be, and she was determined to have a good quarrel about this. "You who have disgraced yourself and got all the neighbours looking down their noses at us. You who have been hanging about with one of those filthy gipsies, and we who have always been proud people, and have held our heads high."

Nothing would stop that shrewish tongue.

Fay had suffered for it through long years of her life, and bitter experience had taught her how it would rasp through this house, and how they would all be made to suffer for it. Her mother was furious about last night, though how she had discovered it Fay did not know. She was one of those women who pushed her nose into almost everything and was determined to find out things. I can't bear it, thought Fay desperately; I cannot go on like this.

Then she saw James Day coming in at the gate, with his handsome wagon standing in the road, for he had fine wagons and kept his horses trim.

"He'll have heard of it like as not," said her mother, grumbling as she worked in the close little kitchen, "and you'll have spoilt your chances for good and all, my girl, and serve you right too."

She went to the door.

Instantly her tongue changed; it became smooth and honeyed; she wiped her hands on the roller towel, and stood there with them folded on her high stomach, and staring out at James as he stood on the step.

He said: "I was wondering if Fay would care to come to the fair along of me this afternoon?" He asked it kindly; she knew by the sound of his voice that he wanted to give her a treat. But somehow she did not want to go near the fair ground again. She felt something tugging in her heart and warning her to keep away. She did not think that she could bear it if she met Noah up there, or saw his mother in her van telling fortunes.

"She'd be pleased," her mother was saying, accepting it as though it were her own invitation.

Fay could do nothing.

James was saying: "Things start getting a bit lively about four o'clock, and then I'd call for her and we'd walk up to the field together. It's amusing up there. I'm a good shot on cocoa-nuts," and he laughed.

"It's very good of you," said Mrs. Denvers,

and her sharp little eyes were studying his face. She had never thought that one of her girls would look so high as the miller, with his two fields, and his handsome mill, even though his first wife might have hanged herself on the tarnished willow tree alongside. It meant that there would be free flour and pig food for her family, and she would expect Fay to do things for her in return for the things that she had done for Fay when she was too little to see after herself.

"I'll see she's ready in time," said Mrs. Denvers; "I'm sure it's most kind of you."

James still lingered, hoping to catch sight of the girl, but Mrs. Denvers knew better than to allow that to happen. She realized that Fay might make excuses, and she was anxious that the afternoon's project should come off. She bid James goodbye, and watched him turn out of the little yard and round the path by the water butt to the gate where his handsome wagon stood.

Then she turned back to Fay.

"I can't go, Mother."

"You're going, my gel. Let them that are older and wiser make up your mind for you. After last night I wonder you aren't ashamed to say such things."

" But how can I go? He might be there."
She was forced to say it.

" And if he is there, it's no notice of him you
will be taking! Let him realize that he forgot
himself daring to speak to a girl from the village,
show him his place, and let him stay in it.
That's how you will treat him, and then perhaps
he'll learn. He ought to, anyway."

But her mother did not understand the darkness of his eyes and the warmth of his mouth.
She did not realize the physical attraction which
lay with Noah, and his way of speech and the
song that he sang. It seemed to Fay to be almost
too much to ask to believe that once her mother
had been in love, and once she and her father
had stood together in a springtime lane, looking
lovingly into one another's eyes. Today those
eyes were sharply shrewish, today those hands
were almost too ready to smack difficult children, and to check and to control. Once she supposed there must have been romance, when the
two of them had wooed in the lane which ran
through the village and on and up to the big
bypass.

It is always hard for girls to believe that once
their mothers were Juliets and their fathers
Romeos, but this is the way that the world goes
on!

All day storm railed through the cottage.

Her father was busy with the ewes, and he would not be back from the lambing yard until late. In some ways Fay was sorry, because she liked her father, and respected his judgment, and sometimes he would check the raillery of his wife's tongue, and forbid her to go on nagging at the children. Not often, for in the wear and tear of years he had learnt his place. He never interfered if he could help it. Today he had foreseen that there might be struggle, and although the ewes did not really need him there, for their time was hardly come, he sat comfortably down amongst the pleasant straw, and ate his dinner there, and grinned to think that he had left his wife to her own devices.

The shepherd boy, who helped, asked him why he laughed, and he turned a grinning face to him.

"Some folks laugh at what they've got," he said; "but I'm laughing at what I've missed."

The boy said nothing. He knew quite well that sometimes the shepherd talked that way, and wondered if it was the way the moon was turning, or if he really had some hidden meaning which the lad could not understand.

In the middle of the afternoon the wind brought the first sound of the music from the fair ground. It was a familiar tune which had run the gamut of cheap gramophones, of radio, and had been whistled by every errand boy in London. The first notes called the loafers up towards the fair field, as they were expected to do. And then the girls who were idle at home, and one or two of the wives who were not expecting their husbands back until late.

"You'll be making yourself smart," said her mother, calling up the cheap box staircase to her daughter.

"All right, Mother."

"Your best things, and no nonsense. I want my gel to be the sort of gel a man can be proud of. If Mr. Day is good enough to take you out, you'll do him credit. Your best Sunday things."

"It looks like rain," she protested. From the lattice window, where in summer a red rose curled and in autumn the grey froth of Old Man's Beard fluffed graciously round it, she could see the dark clouds smearing the sky.

"Go along with you! You'll risk that. The new green coat and skirt that you bought and the hat with violets on it which was for Easter Sunday."

"Very well."

With a heavy heart, Fay brought them out of their boxes, kept under the mattress which she shared with her sisters. She put them on. There was some joy in the finery, but her heart was heavy with apprehension as to what she would do if she got to the fair and met Noah. He would be sure to be there. He would be sure to see her. If she saw him she would want to break away from James Day and explain what had happened. Tonight, she promised herself, she would get down to the barn somehow or other, and she knew that he would be there too. Tonight, even if it meant that there was a worse quarrel than ever in the home, she would pretend that James had asked her to his house, and she would go out apparently for that reason. She would slip inside the barn and make sure that nobody saw. She would not run the gamut of village gossip again; she would be more careful. Last night in the wet and the rain, and with people dispirited from the fair being so unsuccessful, she had never thought that perhaps she might be seen. This time she would think, and she would be sure.

She liked the look of herself in the new green coat and skirt with the white blouse which was as good as silk, yet half the price. She liked the way the leghorn hat with the violets on it fitted well down on to her head. It made her eyes look bluer, and her hair more golden.

If Noah saw her like this, surely he would be pleased with her? Surely he would like the look of her?

"Now are you nearly ready? I can hear him coming up the street, and I wouldn't have you keep him waiting," her mother screamed up the stairs. "I don't know what you do hanging about all this time."

"I'm coming, Mother."

She went down the stairs, and she knew that her new shoes hurt and that she felt depressed even if she were going out with James for the first time, and even if she might meet Noah. At the foot of the stairs, in the tiny hall, where you could hardly open the front door without hitting the lowest stair, her mother was waiting. The shrewd eyes took in everything.

"Well, you look all right, I must say. He ought to be pleased with you. Now, no nonsense, my gel. You realize that he is a man the whole village has run after, and a fine husband he'll make, and a good father. What's more, I shan't expect you to forget your poor old mother, and your brothers and sisters when that time comes. Don't you think it."

"I shan't forget."

It wouldn't be possible, she knew. If her mother succeeded in marrying her to James

Day, it was perfectly obvious that she would expect pickings, and would see that she got them.

He was waiting by the gate. She had always thought that he looked a fine man, even though it struck her that he was old. Tall, well built, and wide with it. But today he looked heavy; he did not walk with the airiness of Noah, who had the gipsies' walk, and she found that she was comparing the two men. One was youth and romance, the other was something far more solid.

It had been raining, and the earth smelt fresh, and the wallflowers growing in the tiny front garden between the house and the privet hedge were fragrant with sweetness.

He glanced at her shoes.

"You mustn't be spoiling your nice new shoes," he said.

"They hurt."

"Then why do you wear them?"

"My mother thought you'd like them."

He stood there staring down at the silly little fancy shoes, which she had saved up to buy. "They're pretty," he said, "but walking round a fair takes a long time, and you walk a good many miles. Slip back and put on your old shoes. May as well start comfortable."

"I don't think Mother will like it."

"Meaning you are frightened of her?"

"Oh no," she said quickly, because she thought that there would be some disgrace in admitting anything of the sort. "It isn't that I'm frightened; she is a good mother, and she cares for all of us."

"Then you slip back and change the shoes."

She was grateful that he should think about her that way, and she went back. Her mother was peeling potatoes for the evening meal, and she looked up sharply.

"Not back already? I never met such a girl."

"He sent me back to change my shoes."

"Whatever for?"

"They hurt."

The older woman tossed her head and went on peeling the potatoes, and dropping them into the water with a plop. "When I was young I learnt that pride felt no pain. I'd have been thankful to have a smart pair of shoes to go to the fair in, but girls have changed, and times have changed. Not for the better, neither."

Fay went upstairs, changed the shoes, and came down again. James was till waiting at the gate, pulling at a pipe.

"That's better," he said.

They walked up the village street side by side, and saying nothing. She felt uncomfortable;

he felt satisfied in that he had persuaded her to come out with him. He did not think that there was any need for words, and was unaware of her embarrassment. Eyes were cocked from behind curtains, and across short blinds. It was something in the nature of a piece of gossip, because they knew what it indicated when a man took a girl for a walk down the street. Mrs. Denvers had long been bragging about the fact that James had looked at her second daughter, and they had accepted it as so much exaggeration. But this looked as though matters were materializing. They nodded together.

The two went to the end of the village, past the barn where last night so much seemed to have happened, and up the hill again to the fair. As they drew nearer they could hear the music, and the laughter of the people in the swing boats, and the heavy thuds of those who were throwing for cocoanuts.

"We'll go the round," said James; "do it all."

"All" meant Haidee and her fortune-telling.

"I'd like a cocoanut," said Fay.

"A cocoanut you'll be having."

He stopped at the first shy, where the red, white and blue had run ignominiously on the cocoanut stands. An oaf of a boy mechanically handed him four balls and charged threepence for them.

"Here goes," said James.

He threw straight.

He had been a practised shot for years, and the first ball hit a cocoanut a shattering blow, but left it in its stand. The same thing happened with another.

"Hi," said James, "those cocoanuts! Have you glued them in?"

The boy appeared indifferent.

The third ball did the same thing. Before the boy could stop him, James had marched across the short piece of green to the stands himself. With his two hands he tried to wrest a cocoanut out of the iron hoop which held it. It would not come. He turned to the boy.

"What about this?" he asked.

"That's fair! You don't have to pick 'em out; you knocks 'em out."

"Nothing would get them out. They're too firmly stuck in! Look."

Fay stood back amongst the little crowd which had come up. She had to admit that she admired James at this moment. He towered above the others, and he did not lose his temper. He did not bluster. The men who ran the cocoanut shy clustered round him gesticulating, but his coolness won them over. He took his time.

Finally he emerged with three cocoanuts in his arms to join her again.

"That didn't frighten you?"

"No," she said.

It was curious that she hadn't been frightened, because usually she hated scenes. Today she had not minded because James had a way of carrying off the affair.

"Here's a cocoanut for you, not won by the right means, but we'll try again later on. Would you care to see the dwarfs?"

"Yes, please."

The dwarfs were in an adjacent tent. Five queer little people, with grotesquely big heads and absurd small fat feet and hands, who sat together on a form and stared at their audience. The whole scene was lit by a flare. One by one they did their turns, mechanically, as though it were of no possible interest to them. They walked on their hands; they turned somersaults; they danced; and the girl from the far corner sang.

They made Fay feel miserable, because they were so grotesque, and she was quite glad when they came out into the open again.

"You didn't like them?" he asked.

"It must be awful to be born that way."

"Yes, quite awful! We who have our wits and our bodies never know how much we have to be grateful for. We aren't ever thankful enough."

They went to a rifle booth next and shot little celluloid balls which danced in spray. He won prizes, and let her choose. A big black cat with a thick tassel tail; he said it would bring her luck. Boxes of cheap chocolates, with gaudy pictures of red roses and smiling girls on the lids. He heaped her arms up.

They rode on the galloping horses, in one of the little cars first, because she was afraid, and then he persuaded her to come on to one of the big yellow horses, which rose and fell on corrugated brass bars as they did their circuit. She was amazed to find that she liked it. The colour had come to her cheeks, and she was excited.

They went to the hoop-la, and flung rings. James won a gift here and there, small trinkets for her, more boxes of the execrable chocolates, then he turned abruptly.

"Let's get your fortune told," he said, and took her arm as though to urge her forward.

She found that they were standing before the van where old Haidee was telling her crystal.

XI

For a chance to make your little much?
　　To gain a lover and lose a friend,
　Venture the tree and a myriad such
　When nothing you mar but the year can mend.
　　But a last leaf—fear to touch!
　　　　　　　　ROBERT BROWNING.

FAY knew that this was the moment that she had
dreaded all along, this was the one thing that she
had feared. The van was freshly painted from
its winter hibernation, the wheels shone and
the scarlet hubs looked almost like red eyes staring at her. Smoke curled out of the tiny chimney, and through the open door she could see
Haidee herself. The dark face was smiling at
her, and it struck Fay that there was something
wicked about the black eyes, and the way that
the hair was looped back over the ears in which
chandelier earrings fell.

There were corals at her throat, those wedding corals set in brass, and fine lace, and a scarf
on which red roses and convolvulus twined together.

"I tell truthfully," she was saying; "I know
what the future has for you. I know."

This was the moment that James had wanted
most of all. He was peculiarly superstitious.
When he had lost his first wife he had blamed

it on a fortune that he had himself been told
years ago. He wanted to know if it were written
in the stars that he and this girl would walk together through life.

" Let's have some?" he suggested.

Fay hung back.

" No. No, I'd much rather not."

" Oh, but that is nonsense! Of course you
want your fortune told. It's only a bit of fun."

He was all for pushing his way up the steps
that Noah had made last winter.

Haidee opened the door wide on top, and
begin to waft them upwards with undulating
movements of her hands.

" I will tell you the truth, only the truth,"
she was saying.

" Come along," said James.

Still she hung back.

" I don't believe in such things."

Haidee leaned forward.

She said : " I will make you believe. I will tell
you of everything that has happened in the
past, and by my truthfulness with the past you
shall know that I will speak the truth of your
future."

" Yes, but I'd rather not."

" Oh, come on," said James again.

There seemed to be no hanging back.   He

had pushed her gently up the wooden steps, and now here she was in the van itself. This was Noah's mother. Fay surveyed her. Smaller than she had expected, and yet about her that dignity, that bearing which was unmistakable. She sat down beside the small table with the crystal set upon it. There seemed to be something ominous about the crystal, with its cloudy thickness, and the way that those swarthy hands touched it.

"I don't want my fortune told," said Fay; but her voice had become small in its protests.

"I'll wait," said James.

"You sit outside; it's warm on the steps," said Haidee. "It's all right there!"

Fay wanted to cry, "Don't leave me alone with her; please don't leave me alone with her," but she could not make a sound. It seemed too silly, for there was no reason in this. She sat down opposite Haidee.

The gipsy drew the crystal closer. She laid Fay's hands upon it. Above them she set her own, and now she was looking keenly at the girl, as though she would wrest every secret from her. Fay had the feeling that she knew about last night. She had the idea that her mind was an open book to this woman and she could keep nothing from her.

But for the moment Haidee did not betray herself.

She said: "He is not your lover. You don't care for him. He brought you here against your will; what is more, he brought you to the fair against your will. He is not your sort. He is too old."

It was all perfectly true.

Slowly Haidee lifted her hands from where they lay on the crystal, becoming smeared with contact, and she stared down into it.

She said: "He has been married before, and his wife died. She died by her own hand, and it wasn't poison. I can see that she died. He will marry again. He wants to marry again because he finds life so lonely. You know that?"

"I guessed it," she said.

Haidee turned her eyes again to the crystal, with the steam dying off it, so that now it showed the cloudy depth which Fay could not analyse. She had always thought that a crystal should be clear.

"So," said Haidee, and she took a deep intake of breath as though she had recognized the beginning of some story.

Fay knew what had happened.

"There is another man," said Haidee slowly;

"you met him only a few hours ago. He is smallish and dark, and it was love at first sight. He is different from you, and you are different from him. He is of a strange people. However much you love him, that love can never bring you happiness, true happiness, because your two roads lie so far apart. You think you can have him—you can't!"

She lifted her eyes from the crystal itself. She knows, thought Fay.

Haidee went on.

"That man is going away, right away. He goes for a very long time. He will leave you with a memory sharp as a sword. It will cut as a sword. It will cut through your life if you are not careful. Leave him now before he hurts you too much."

Fay knew that her colour was going. She said: "How do you know?"

The old woman made no further pretence. She folded her two hands over the crystal, as though shutting out some ugly sight.

"He is my son," she said.

There was no sound, save the slight stirring of James on the steps that Noah had made, and the slowing down of the roundabout whilst the man changed the tune. Then it blared forth again, more metallic than ever.

"I have two other sons," said Haidee, "but none of them are like Noah, whom I bore last. Noah will succeed me when I die and my van is burnt. He will live as I have lived, and his wife will be a gipsy girl, and his children will be all of our tribe."

"What about me?"

"He loves you now. He will love you strongly and for ever, perhaps more than he loves his wife, but you are not the woman that he will marry." She patted the crystal as though it were some child. She did not need to look into it any longer, because now the future was clear to her. "He will always love you, but for that love he will lie," she said, "and he will come back here, back where he belongs, back where his own need him."

"But me—what happens to me?"

Haidee shifted her hands uneasily upon the smoothness of the crystal. "You will have children, three of them; you will have a good, kind husband, and you will never look back. The day will come when you will be glad that you did not marry here, when you recognize that it could not have been. That is the truth."

"What is the lie?" she asked.

"I don't know," said Haidee.

She was staring at the girl, with those dazzling

eyes of hers which were blackbird bright. She
was thinking in her heart how she detested the
paleness that had attracted Noah, those eyes,
which were like the Cornish sea that mild September morning when she had bathed there.
She had been young then, and had believed in
the pixies and the fairies which hover about that
Cornish coast. The sea had been so tempting.
But when she had touched it, it had chilled her
through, and she thought of these blue eyes in
the same way: tempting, but cold.

She said: "You will never marry him. That
I swear by everything that I know, and of the
future I know much. It is the truth."

Fay was suddenly stung to insistence.

She said: "Last night, when my people said
it was impossible, I thought it was. Now when
you say it is impossible I know that you are
wrong. Quite wrong. I *will* marry him, you'll
see."

She got up. At this particular moment she
had an extraordinary sense of power. She believed that she had the upper hand, yet when she
looked into the calmly penetrating eyes of the
gipsy she was not sure. She was aware that her
own eyes betrayed her, whereas those dark, glit-
tering eyes hid secrets.

"As you will," said Haidee indifferently.

" But time will show you that it is I who am right, and you who are wrong. Much water will pass down the river, and many suns will shine on the valley, but in a few years you will look back to this moment and you will know that my son rules the tribe, and that the children you hold in your arms are the children of another man."

She got up, significant of dismissal. Fay stumbled out of the van, and went awkwardly down the steps, where James was waiting.

" It's my turn now," he said, and, before she could stop him, was halfway up the steps that she had found so difficult of negotiation. She turned quickly and caught at his coat.

" Please, James, don't go. She is so queer. She . . . she almost frightens me."

" She'll find she can't frighten me! She'll find that she can't tell me anything that'll scare me. No, we said we'd do the lot, and it is the lot that we'll do! Then we will compare fortunes; who knows that there might be something in the two?"

He had gone inside the jaunty little door; she could see him settling down before the table, with the crystal between him and Haidee. She could only wait. She stood there embarrassed and awkward, rather angry with him for having gone definitely against her, and insisting on having his fortune told. She did not know what to do.

Then she knew that Noah was at hand. She knew it without hearing him come, because he had the art of walking without sound, the art which is born in the tribe, and part of the urgent necessity of living.

He was standing there, in his old tweed coat, with the clean shirt that had no collar but showed his throat dark, and rounded, and muscular.

"Well?" he said.

Helplessly she tried to cover her embarrassment. "I didn't expect you'd be here."

"I live here."

"Yes, of course," she said, and only hoped that her voice sounded natural; it did not feel like it.

"Tonight, you'll come to the barn?" he asked gently, and she recognized the longing in his tone. "I have much to tell you. I'm not going on with this kind of life, but breaking free. I went to see the gentleman this morning. It's all fixed."

"You're not leaving the tribe?"

"Yes, I am. Now don't make a noise! We don't want them to hear yet. They mustn't

know. But it is you that I shall tell tonight.
You'll be there, about the same time?"

"Yes, I'll be there."

"You had your fortune told?"

She nodded, hoping that he would not ask
her what Haidee might have said, and he recognized this, for he did not say any more, just stood
there, looking at her with those soft, dark eyes
of his, which had none of his mother's beadi-
ness and shrewdness, but were romantically
loving.

Presently she said: "You mustn't stay here.
My friend is having his fortune done, and he'll
be down before long."

"I see."

He did not argue. He merely turned and
went back to the shooting booth which he had
been minding with Zilla.

Then she waited.

Later James came down the steps well pleased
with himself, and she knew that he had liked his
fortune, and that Haidee must have flattered
him.

"Good things coming," he said, and was so
cheered that he linked his arm in hers and drew
her through the crowd, which was thickening by
this time. The people had come from the village drawn by the music and the laughter, and

soon the flares would be lit which would draw more.

"What did she tell you?"

"She told me that I would marry the maid of my heart, and that I'd have three children, three fine children, and live to be old. She told me about the mill, and the past. She *knew* the past."

"She couldn't have known it."

He said: "Strange things are written in those crystals, and she knew every one of them. She knew about Violet."

It was the first time that he had mentioned his wife, and Fay did not know why, but it gave her a strange feeling. "She couldn't have known about her," she repeated slowly.

"She did know. She told me of our marriage. It wasn't happy. I sometimes think that the whole thing was my fault, and that we ought to have split rather than let matters go on to that horrible end, but she did not want to split. She was a queer girl and she had strange dreams. She ought not to have married. That was about the truth of it, poor lass."

He said it considerately, and she guessed that he had been through a bad time, that he had suffered with his wife, and that he was hiding his share, and dwelling on the point that he had

not understood her, and that he should have
been better to her.

"I'm sure you were goodness itself to her,"
she said, because he was a good man, and she
knew that he would be kind and considerate
and would do his best for a wife.

"It's easy to blame yourself after. I was busy
with the mill at the time. It was the year of
those bad floods, and I was singlehanded. It's
no good worrying about things now, no good
thinking about them—what's done is done; the
thing to do is to make better progress in the
future."

She said yes.

They walked through the fair, he with his
arms full of cocoanuts and prizes that they had
won, and she carrying the big black cat with the
fluffy tail, which would do well for Doris, who
would be mightily well pleased with it. The
villagers looked at them, nudged one another,
and whispered that "maybe it was a case" and
"anyway, she wouldn't be doing too badly for
herself."

They walked to the edge of the fair field, with
the sunset lying across the valley, too lemon-
green, too streaked with watery cloud, to bode
well. It would rain again before long, for the
distance was clear as a piece of needlework, as

though it were but a mile to the hills, when it was all five miles. The village belfry looked as though you could reach out and touch it with your two hands.

They said little, there did not seem to be any need for words, and James was thinking of the future, and the day when he could press his suit home, and all the gipsy had said about his pale blonde wife and the three handsome children that she would bear him. Fay was thinking back into the past. She was wondering about Violet, the whimsical and imaginative creature who had hanged herself on the tarnished willow alongside the mill.

She did not think that she could ever fancy living there, as her mother had suggested, because that willow tree would be like a signpost, pointing to the crossroads whence poor Violet had come, and had taken the wrong turning. And, even if the creature had been demented, it had been a tragedy just the same, and there must have been suffering and agony of mind and apprehension. All those emotions would live like ghosts in the mill, and surely they would haunt the woman who came to dwell there, as Violet had once dwelt, bride of James.

No, it was a good thing that she was going to marry Noah when the time came.

They returned to the gate of home, and she did not know whether to ask James in. If she did and her mother were caught unawares, there would be sharpness and anger after, and if she did not ask him in, there would be sharpness and anger just the same, seeing that her mother would feel that she had missed an opportunity.

Doris and Eileen came running out, and between them poor little Jimmy, who had no roof to his mouth, and could not talk properly, but, as Fay very well knew, was the nicest of the family.

"What have you brought?" screamed the girls, and Jimmy stood there making queerly inarticulate noises, and pointing at the black cat with the big tassel of a tail.

She knelt down to give it to him, there on the clay path, even though it would mark her new suit because the clay was not dry yet from the rain.

She turned to James. "He can't speak properly, you know, and he values things so much. I hope you don't mind?" She had meant to give it to Doris, but somehow she couldn't. Doris would not care for it as Jimmy would, and Jimmy got so little. She watched him running round the path by the water butt lop-sidedly, because his feet went strangely, and seemed to run away with him so that he resembled a spider.

"You're good to him," said James. "I like that in you. You're good to him."

"Thank you so much for taking me to the fair."

"Perhaps on Sunday you will let me take you for a walk?" he volunteered, rather bashfully.

She wanted to say no, but could not think how to do so when already he had been so kind to her.

"We'll see when Sunday comes," she said.

Then, before he could argue about it, and put her in a difficult position, she turned and went along the path to the back door after Jimmy.

XII

And there shall be for thee all soft delight,
That shadowy thought can win,
A bright torch, and a casement ope at night,
To let the warm Love in!

KEATS.

FAY ought to have known that it wouldn't be easy to get away the second night. Although her mother was intensely pleased at the success of James's taking Fay to the fair, and although she contemplated with pleasure the cocoanuts, and the cheap little prizes, and Jimmy on the old sofa fondling the cat with the black tassel of a tail, she was at the same time suspicious.

The rain came soon after the sunset, a heavy storm which must have washed out the fair for the time being, and ruined it for the second night. The storm gave a little later, but it was an eerie night with few stars.

Doris and Eileen came up to bed early. Doris she could rely upon to fall asleep, but Eileen was usually difficult. Tonight, however, Eileen felt queer and rolled on to the mattress and was half asleep almost before her sister could speak.

Fay waited.

She knew that her mother and father would be unlikely to come up to see her again. Bert had been a trouble. He had been out snaring rabbits with the other boys and had caught a pheasant. One of the keepers must have seen him because he had come round to the back door just as Fay was going up to bed. The trouble with the keeper had diverted her mother's attention, and there was a screeching argument going on. She and her father were waiting up for Bert's return, when he would receive due punishment, because the keeper had said that a case was pending. Sir Edmond Stewart, to whom the ground belonged, had been wanting to make an example of somebody all this spring. He had been well aware that a band of village boys were poaching and only wanted the chance to bring them to book. This chance had now offered itself.

Mrs. Denvers and her husband had been amused when the pheasant had appeared at the cottage, bulging inside Bert's jacket. They had cooked it and had enjoyed the meal, but now, when they saw trouble looming ahead, they were all against Bert.

This would keep them busy.

When Bert returned, quite possibly with further booty, there would be the usual raucous argument, and his father's belt for him.

It looked as though the stars were kindly.

Fay dared not go downstairs. She opened the lattice window and she saw that the rain had abated a good deal; now it was merely spotting and she would need little more than a coat. Many a time she had climbed out this way, and down on to the top of the shed; she could slither down the corrugated iron and on to the ground, and nobody would be any the wiser. Doris would not waken; she was a good child and slept heavily and late. She doubted if Eileen would be disturbed again tonight; she had looked too seedy.

Now she ran out of the garden and down the

lane. Nobody was about. Last night she would have thought that all the gossips were home and still could not imagine how she had been seen, but tonight she was cautious.

They had had their soaking at the fair, and they would be glad of their firesides, for the wind blew chilly, and the rain had had a smattering of hail in it.

She ran up the road, keeping well under the lee of the hedge. She turned into the farmyard, just as deserted, just as silent, save for the noise of a horse grating against its manger chain, and the grunt of the pigs nuzzling amongst the stale straw in their yard.

She opened the little door set inside the big one of the barn. It was dark inside, and warm. There came the pleasant scent of the hay, and of the corn cake that was stocked there for the cattle.

She could not see in the dimness. Nervously she hesitated.

She was suddenly afraid; she dared not go forward, yet was reluctant to go back.

Then she heard a stir.

"I'm here," said Noah.

She could see nothing.

Arms drew her gently inside the warm darkness of the barn. She felt his breath upon her cheek, knew that she walked forward towards the hay and that he pressed her gently down upon it. This was a dream. Nothing else that had happened mattered. The cottage had faded, and the mother with her clattering tongue, and the bedroom with the fetid air and the three of them lying there on the old tired mattress. This was something worth living a whole lifetime for!

"I'm going away," he said.

"The fair leaves tomorrow?"

"Yes, but I leave tonight. Late. That gentleman is taking me to London, getting me trained, making something great of me. I'm going right away, and I'll be back in a year's time. When the fair comes again to the field I'll be back, but I'll be rich then, I'll be a famous man, and you'll be proud to marry me. It won't be a gipsy wedding, but a white one in a real church. You'll make a lovely bride."

And he kissed her.

It was a dream, she kept telling herself; it was something that she could not believe had happened. It was real, vital: the impossible had happened.

Then she remembered the year between.

"How will I live it?" she asked.

"Of course you'll live it."

"They want me to marry James Day."

" The man who came to Haidee with you this afternoon? Of course you cannot marry him; he is old."

He spoke with the contempt of youth, which looks at the mid-thirties as though it were grey and bent, and walked with a lagging step.

" He is very kind."

" You don't marry because a man is kind, but because you love him. You and I loved the moment that we met. We knew one another. Just as though we had been born in another world and had loved before. We loved again. You know that is so."

" Yes."

He said : " One little year to wait, then I will be back. I will come on the morning of next year's fair, and you will be glad that you waited, glad to see me. I will take you away with me then, and make you my own."

" But supposing it takes longer than a year?" she asked.

" I will come back. I promise you that I'll come back. Wait for me. Keep faith. Be strong in standing out against a man who is only kind. I will come back."

Listening to him she was quite sure of it; quite sure that he would come back to her and that he would make her his own.

"Your voice is so beautiful that I know Mr. Richard will make you great," she said.

"I'll sing for all the world," he promised her.

Now he too was exhilarated.

Somehow, sitting here in the hay with the barn rising above them like a vaulted roof, fame seemed to be within their grasp. All the difficulties seemed to be smoothed away. And where once Fay had thought that the year would be an eternity, now she saw it as a passage of time which would go fast. She would get a place away, she would escape from the cottage which was a prison, and next spring she would come back to the fair again and meet him.

"But supposing you don't come?" she whispered, suddenly afraid.

"I shall come. There is, of course, just the chance that I might not be rich and famous enough, that I might still be training, but you can be sure that I shall come the moment I am free."

"So many men must have promised that to girls at so many times," she faltered.

He took her hand in his. "See," he said, "I will swear by this hand. I will swear by my faith. I will swear by all that I hold dear, and I will keep my word."

He kissed her wrist, and the tips of her fingers, and finally her lips.

She cried: " I want to believe you so much; something in me does believe you. At the same time everything that I have ever learnt tells me that it would be so easy for you to go away for ever."

"I will teach you other things. Things that the people who live under roofs do not teach their children. I will teach you that the word given in solemn promise is the bond. I will come back."

Frantically she clung to him. It seemed that they had known one another for a long time; it was not just the friendship, rapidly drifting into lovership, of two people who had but recently met. She felt that they had know one another all their lives, she felt that they could not be separated, and that he would return some day.

"I shall never care for anyone else," she protested.

"I know, my sweet, I know."

"Promise me you will come back? I will fight the world for you. You don't know what my mother is; you don't know what life can be here in this rotten little village where everybody talks, but I'll fight it all if only you will come back to me?"

"I will come back," he promised.

There was no need to panic. No need at all. Suddenly sitting here that peace seemed to descend upon them both, the peace which brings with it the promise of security. She did not need to doubt his word.

Time passed. She forgot Doris and Eileen asleep at home, and the trouble downstairs with Bert. She forgot that the clock was telling the hours her absence might have been discovered. Much later, hand in hand, they slipped out of the barn, and now she knew that she thought of it as being something sacred, much as she thought of the little church with its squat belfry, and its yew trees flanking it, like so many nuns, drawing their hoods closer about them.

They passed out into the yard, lit by the brilliant moonlight, for the storm clouds had gone. The manger chain still grated, and the pigs still rootled amongst the stale straw, but hand in hand these two passed out of the gate, and into the country lane.

He said: "I go this way, and my path leads to fame. I will come back for you and you shall tread the same path. Fame will come for you too."

"Noah, I shall die if you don't return."

"You won't die, because I shall return."

He kissed her again; then she watched him walk away. He walked with that long, easy gait. He walked, and as he went he sang. It was the song of the rain on a silver road when storms come, of the sun on the new green leaves of spring, and the red and gold leaves of autumn. It was the song that all the gipsies know.

XIII

Oh, what were best to roam, or rest?
On land's lap or the water's breast,
To sleep on yellow millet-sheaves
Or swim in the lucid shallows just,
Eluding water-lily leaves.
An inch from Death's black fingers thrust
To lock you, when release he must.
What life were best on summer eves?
                                    ROBERT BROWNING.

Now, quite suddenly, Fay knew that it was very late indeed. As she sped down the lane, still wet and slippery from the rain, though lit by the moon which had struggled out and had overcome the clouds, she heard the church clock striking in the belfry. She had no idea that time had gone so fast.

Brought back to reality with a jerk, she panicked and felt her heart making a disturbed noise within, and knew that she must get home quickly, and hide the fact that she had been away.

As she turned the corner of the lane and saw all the little houses clustering together, all dark, to show that their occupants had already gone to bed, she noticed a little apart that a light burned in the white cottage which was her home.

The moment that she saw that light she was afraid. Her people were hard and stern. They abided by a certain set of morals. Already they had been angered about Bert, and if they had discovered her absence, seeing that they would have a very good idea with whom it had been spent, they would be indignant.

Last night she had evaded punishment on the grounds that she was too old. She would not be so lucky a second time. Her father believed in the use of his belt, because that was the way that he himself had been brought up. Her mother would not take her part. There had been too much trouble in her own family, for in her youth she had had a sister who had come home looking wan and pale, and who had presented the family with a lusty son. She had no wedding ring.

The mother believed that such vices ran in families, and that the only way to cure such girls and to make sure of no repetition was by fear.

Fay's legs weakened, and she thought that she would drop. For one frenzied moment she had a thought of running back to the vans, of finding Noah and asking him to take her with him. She could not bear to face the agony if she had been discovered. Then she remembered the old gipsy bending over her crystal, and knew that she would get but scant sympathy there. They had no welcome for a girl born of other tribes, for a girl who had slept repeatedly under a roof. She would not be wanted.

She opened the gate quite silently, and tiptoed up the path to the shed. She went up the roof as she had come, nimbly, because she was young and agile. The corrugated iron was slippery and she had to be very careful, coming to the window at last, and levering herself through it.

Doris lay there curled up asleep quite oblivious, but Eileen was awake, and turned heavy eyes towards the window.

"So you're back?" she said, and her voice croaked with illness.

"Hush! Yes, I'm back."

"You'll catch it! Mother's been up here."

Again there was the feeling that her legs would not carry her. She began feverishly to unbutton her frock, wondering if she could brave it out and pretend that her mother had suffered from an hallucination, and that she had been here all the time.

It was useless.

Her mother must have heard her come in, or Eileen speaking, for Fay could hear her stumping up the stairs, and the door opened again, admitting a tousled head.

" So you've troubled yourself to come home?"

The good intentions fluttered away, like so many brave banners suddenly draggled into the mud. She said nothing. She could not bluster out the situation; she was too young.

"You'd better come on down," said her mother, and jerked her head in the direction of the room below.

" I haven't got my frock on."

"You won't want your frock on for what's coming to you," she said, and laughed. There was something hideous about her laugh.

Fay had gone numb.

She did not know how her legs carried her down the box stairs—she, who only half an hour ago had been in Noah's arms in the sweetness of the hay. A woman then, a woman deeply and irrevocably in love, and now just a girl, treated humiliatingly as a child.

They passed through the front room which

was never used, with its stuffed bird in a glass case, and the wax fruit that had been Grandma's, and the slippery, shiny chairs, and the crochet mat on the table. In the kitchen the fire had burnt low, and the place smelt of oil from the lamp, and dead ashes. Her father looked ominous.

They had had a difficult evening, because they knew that Bert was in for trouble, and it looked very much as though he were not the only one in the family.

"You've been out with that gipsy lad again?" said her father.

"Yes."

"I told you not to. No good could come of it. Gipsies are treacherous."

"But he isn't, he isn't," she said. "He is gentle, and he is kind. He is going away to become a great singer—Mr. Richard from the vicarage is taking him—and one day he will come back to marry me. He says so. He will come back."

"Maybe somebody will need to marry you before then," sneered her mother; "we had that with my sister Lily, and it looks as if we were going to have it again in this house. I told you last night what 'ud be coming to you if you went on that way. Well, now you'll get it. Big gel or no big gel, you'll have to be treated the same way."

Fay groped on to the table edge and stood there staring at them both. Her mother with her querulous little face screwed up, and her accusing, hard little eyes, her father undoing his belt.

"I've done nothing wrong," she protested; "I only talked to him. He's coming back to marry me. He is, really. I've done nothing wrong."

"You've disobeyed your father and your mother, who knows best for you," said Mrs. Denvers, "and them that disobeys must learn what happens. You give it her, Father. Maybe then she'll learn to stay at home and not go off after them dirty gipsies."

She went out of the room.

At that particular moment Fay could think only of Noah. She was living still so much in a dream that she had one staggering idea that he might come in at the door and save her. She could not believe that stark reality was going to overtake the loveliness of those hours in the barn with him. She stared at her father across the little table with last Sunday's paper on it, and the bad-smelling lamp, and the bundle of her mother's mending.

"I did no wrong," she said stupidly.

He ignored that.

"You come along over here, my gel," he said.

Noah had gone home. For him the moon-light painted the world with a silver brush, and he saw ahead of him all within his grasp. Because he had meant every word that he had said, and he would come back to her, he would return to this village in a year's time and he would claim Fay as his own.

Gipsies do not love twice.

He had never fancied one of the olive-skinned girls which his mother wanted for him. Now there was nothing to do but to put together his belongings, which were not many, and start for London in the morning. He knew where to meet Mr. Richard, and the sooner he started on his travels the sooner he would be ready to come back for Fay.

The grass squelched in the meadow, and already many of the booths were down. The swing boats, which had been a gallows-like erection, were laid low. The hoop-las and the shies, which belonged to the gipsies, were all stacked back on the small, fragile-looking little carts, ready to return to the encampment at dawn. But Haidee's van was still lit. He could see the light like a star, and he knew that she realized what had happened and was waiting there.

She wanted to talk to him.

Whatever she said she would not dissuade him from what he meant to do, because his mind was made up, and when he determined upon a thing, nothing would detract him from it. He paused on the brow of the hill and looked back upon the village below. A cluster of little roofs around the belfry. Strange people who slept under those roofs, closed in, like a cage. Strange people who did not understand the loveliness of starry nights, the sharp tang of autumn, the gentle wooing of the spring.

As he stood there he heard the faint sound of a girl screaming.

It was so far away and distant that he ignored it, never associating it with anything in his own life.

He would have slung under the van, but Haidee had heard him, even though he moved quietly, even though he had hoped that he would not be detected. She came to the door of the van. She leant over it and stared down at him.

"You'll be starting early for London?" she said.

He knew that she had strange powers of discernment, but somehow this was more than he had expected.

"How did you know?"

"I just did know."

"Yes, I shall be starting early."

"I never thought that a son of mine would come down to that."

"But I'm going to be famous," he said.

"It isn't famous to sleep under roofs, and to eat your food round a table, and live with men and women who do not understand us and our ways. We áre of the tribe, and you cannot cut yourself free from the tribe."

"I can bring something back to the tribe," he told her. "I am going to sing for the world. You'll see."

"It is no good telling you that happiness does not lie this way? That you'll get all you want save one thing, and that one thing will be the most important of them all? It is the one thing you'll want like hell, but you won't get it."

"I'm getting life."

She leaned lower. "Life, but you won't get your love. Oh no, you won't. I've seen things todays written in my crystal and I know that she'll marry the man who brought her here—be glad to marry him too. You'll get fame, but you won't get her, you fool!"

His mouth had set stubbornly.

"I'm going to try my luck," he said.

"Try your luck and break your heart. Come back here, and you'll be king, but you'll be king without a whole heart. You'll have a wife and gipsy children, pure bred of the tribe, but nothing will make your heart whole again. And this isn't nonsense that I am talking, but truth, as you'll find out, given time."

"My mind's made up," he told her.

"Very well."

She went inside and slammed the door fast. He saw the light die in her window like stars die at dawn. He slung below the van with the others, but he could not sleep. The horses made a noise chafing against the paling they were tied to. His own world seemed to be such an upheaval. He got up early, before the others.

He was almost ready when they stirred and came out to start the work of the day. They did not speak to one another; much had to be done and prepared before they could start, and each man went to his own particular work without asking of the others.

Noah watched them.

Then he hoisted his bundle and saying nothing to any of them started to walk across the field. The fair was level now. Even the grass seemed to have recovered. The roundabout with its handsome steam engine was puffing down the hill towards the road. He hesitated a moment and watched it. It was as though his own life were suddenly moving from him, the whole background changing, the whole scene shifting.

He saw the vans with the lean horses stuck between the shafts, and they turned in a solemn procession with Haidee leading, across the field and out at the gate, turning their heads towards the sea. He saw them go, yellow wheels rotating in the mud and slime churned up by yesterday's fair, one after the other, with the children running alongside, and the noise and the stir about them.

He was no longer part of them.

For a moment he felt lost. He felt as though he had suddenly been zipped out of a picture, and in the new big world had no real part. Then he set his face towards the station, and walked fast so that he might forget.

PART TWO

I

The fruit of my tree of knowledge is plucked, it is
this. Adventures are to the adventurous.—DISRAELI.

LONDON was very different from the city that
Noah had expected. He went round to the
theatre and saw Mr. Richard in a smart office
there. It was all a great deal more splendid
than Noah had expected, and he was intrigued
by it. He wanted this for himself, and believed
that he saw the road clear to getting it. Provided that he did what he was told. For the
moment his whole future depended on being
able to carry out orders.

He found rooms off Covent Garden.

They were professional rooms, high up in a
little garret almost under the stars. He wanted
to be there. He could not have borne the fact
of sleeping low down in a house, with a pile of
bricks and mortar above him, and the knowledge that so much shut out the sky.

"It's high up," the woman said, a large
woman with a pendulous figure, and a big sagging face, though her eyes were kind.

"I don't mind."

He climbed up the stairs from which the lino-
leum had long since been trodden, but was left

here and there in strange wisps of pattern. He thought how much he preferred the wooden steps that he had made for his mother's van last winter, clean and scrubbed, and sweet-smelling, with none of this messiness and no walls to shut him in.

He hated the frowst of the tall house, stuck between a higgledy-piggledy row of houses, the lack of air which was like a thick fog in the hall, the smell of blankets and night-breathing and last week's cooking which came from the floors as he passed them, where families lived clustered together, far worse than any gipsy van.

But the top room of all he liked, if he could ever like a room! It had a pointed ceiling which reminded him in some way of the barn that had smelt of summer. The walls had been washed out with pale cream by some tenant who had found himself unable to bear the ugliness of rose-patterned paper flecked with trellis. The two windows had little green shutters, and there was some remnant of a balcony, so that it was almost like a foreign house. A vine had climbed tediously upwards and had caught at the balcony with green tendrils of fingers, and having once caught hold, now clung.

He saw immediately that he could turn the bed to that balcony, and lie on it with his face

turned up to the stars, so that it would not be
really like sleeping under a roof at all, for his
head would be free.

There was a chest of drawers which had washing accommodation on one side, and some sem-
blance of a dressing-table the other. The boards
were covered with a seedy drugget which had
long ago lost any consistent colour; he could
not tell now whether it had been red, or brown,
or yellow.

Although he liked the room because of the
possibilities of the balcony, he stared at it
mournfully, for he missed the bright colours
that the gipsies adore, he missed the gaiety and
the open air. Then he went to the window,
and sat there, hunched, staring down into the
street below. Covent Garden was alive with
colour. Here were carts with green cabbages
stocked in them, and net sacks of oranges, flar-
ing a brilliant hue against the spring sunshine.
In one corner there was a woman with her arm
full of tulips. Red, and gold, and mauve, all
blurred together, to satisfy the hunger in his
heart.

Yes, I *can* live here, he thought.

He could be nearly happy.

Almost immediately they got him into training. There was far more to this than he had

supposed. He thought that if he applied himself to the work it would not be very long before
he could walk on to some stage and make that
fortune that Mr. Richard had promised him.

Richard showed him to Athelberg, the big
man who owned a chain of theatres, and who relied on Richard to bring novelties to him.

"You shall hear him sing," said Richard.

They went into the dreary theatre, and somebody switched on a light. The mournfulness of
the place like a morgue struck at Noah's heart.
He stumbled across the stage, with the carpets
rolled up, and the scenery standing about.
Trees, drab and ugly, like no trees that he had
ever known. Imitation flowers that would never
look real. He peered down into the maw of the
auditorium and saw the row upon row of empty
stalls, and Athelberg sitting there, knees crossed,
and a flashing white splotch of white spats
showing.

He knew that he could not sing.

He knew that the joy of life and the ecstasy
of freedom which had brought song from him
when he walked beside the van, or poached in
the hedgerows, or lay in the grass blinking up
at the sun—all these were missing.

"Sing, Noah," directed Richard.

He sang, but the trill was not there. It was

not the song of the nightingale in the mating
season, when he woos his beloved, but it was the
song of the nightingale when the beloved has
gone.

Athelberg listened.

Afterwards he discussed the whole matter
with Richard in his office, ornate, thick-car-
peted, with modern furniture absurdly highly
polished.

"The boy has a marvellous compass, I admit
that, but as he is he isn't any good."

"You should have heard him as I heard
him."

"Well, I didn't hear him like that. I heard
what I heard, and I form my own opinion on
that. He is worth spending some money on because I think you've got big stuff there! But
it'll take time."

"What do you propose to do?"

"Put him under Engardine for a bit."

Engardine was a man with long, dark hair,
and eyes in which a fire burnt. Noah discovered
that. He liked him in that Engardine reminded
him of his own people; there had undoubtedly
been gipsy blood in him at some time or other,
but generations ago. He understood music.

In his studio Noah suffered tortures.

He would have thrown it all to the winds of

chance and have gone back to the vans, with their yellow wheels trundling through the mud of country lanes, and over the short, close-clipped grass of heaths; but he felt that if he gave it up he must love Fay, and he would not lose her for all the world.

He would struggle on.

For three solid months he toiled at those exercises in which he could see no rhyme nor reason. For three months he worked early and late, and he did not think he could have borne it, save for the fact that he could sleep with his face upturned to the stars in the strange house which overlooked the Garden.

It was a stifling summer, and he felt the heat badly, because he was so unused to surplus clothes and to the closeness of living under a roof.

He bought new clothes, and wore them.

He was proud of the fact that he could look as smart as any, but irritated that he had to limit the extent of his taste to flamboyant handkerchiefs and ties and to bright shirts. He wore these with an air.

She would be proud of him, he told himself.

At the end of three months he heard himself singing again, and he knew that his voice was richer, that the notes came more easily, that it was not the same voice at all. Athelberg heard him.

There was something about Athelberg that Noah hated. It might be the way that he sat indolently in the empty stalls, smoking that fat cigar of his, staring with pig eyes, his hands folded on his enormous paunch. There was something about Athelberg that could stem the artist in Noah, so that the notes were frustrated, so that he could not trill. But today he refused to be beaten. He would not look at Athelberg. He would think of all those sweetnesses for which he was homesick—the roads with the spring greening the hedges, the lush ditches masked in a fine lace of cow's parsley, the cornfields in August, yellowing, and the rare blue mist of sea horizon at the edge of the cliff.

He sang splendidly.

"You've got a treasure there," said Athelberg, stirred out of his lethargy.

The cigar ash had dripped down his waistcoat and he had not noticed it. He turned quite enthusiastically to Richard beside him.

"I knew he was good."

"So good that we must send him to finer masters."

"What do you mean?"

"People abroad. That chap in Munich—

what's his name, that German professor? He'd produce those top notes; he is a genius in that way. Send him over there for a while. We are on something special here. Maybe a Caruso."

"Maybe," said Richard.

When it was broken to Noah he did not want to go. Munich was so far away. He knew it, of course, because some of the gipsies came from there, and he had himself been to Leipzig Fair and thought of it with the homesick longing of a man who is enduring too much. But now he had become foolishly attached to the frowsty house, with the room where he could lie under the stars. There might come a time when he had to board under a roof, and he did not think that he could bear the thought.

"I can't go," he said.

They persuaded him.

It took some time, because he was not easy to talk round, and they held out the bait of riches. Richard had discovered about Fay, and he told Noah of everything that he would be able to buy for her. He held before him the baubles which can appeal only to that type of mind.

"Very well," said Noah.

He left London and sailed in a cargo boat, because he chose this. He could sleep on deck. Night after night he dossed down on a coil of

rope and lay there, staring up at the stars between the masts, like wise yellow eyes, and growing larger. The farther east he went, the larger
those stars became.

It was like a dream.

Munich was a city shut in by mountains. He
found the old professor, and somehow he liked
him. The professor was dazzled by the boy's
voice. He understood temperament. He arranged a bed for him on the flat roof of the
house where he lived, a little bed that was rolled
up by day, and by night sprawled under a couple
of palms in pots and a straggling rose.

There were times when Noah was able to
wander along the roads which lie around
Munich. He went to the mountains. He met
the travelling tinkers, and the Hungarian gipsies who wander there, he went to fairs, and he
changed.

His voice changed too.

Suddenly he recognized in it the quality that
was entirely different. Before it had been crude,
now it was softening so that the notes were more
like water; before it had been a wild bird singing for ecstasy on a blossom-sweet bough, but
now it was the tinkle of water tossed rhythmic-
ally down some mountain side, and making
music as it fell.

I am going to be great, he said to himself, and knew that it was true.

He must not chafe against time and the struggle to become king of his profession. Before him he set his goal, which was Fay; he set her like a figure in a niche at which saints pray. He thought of her as a blue madonna, with that pale gold hair, and those soft shining eyes, and knew that he would come back to her and lay the spoils of this at her feet.

I love her so much, he said.

But time passed into the matterless; there was so much to be learnt and to be accomplished before he could think of time. He became passionately interested in the production of his voice.

He went on to Prague.

II

Ploughmen, bear in mind
  Your labour is for future hours;
Advance, spare not, nor look behind,
Plough deep and straight with all your powers!
                              R. H. HORNE.

ON that particular night after she had met him in the barn against her parents' wishes, and knowing that she was openly defying them, eventually Fay crept to bed.

Doris still slept, the deep, untrammelled sleep of childhood. Eileen lay there staring with somnolent eyes. She was a strange child who took a delight in defying her sister. She had never cared for Fay, who had sometimes grown impatient having to be saddled with the youngsters in a pram when she herself wanted to play.

Eileen had deliberately told upon her. Fay knew that the moment she returned to the bedroom, dragging her smarting body with her.

Eileen had known where Fay had gone, and had herself told her mother the moment that she could. Then she had lain awake, feeling sick and ill, but feeling some certain comfortable reassurance in the knowledge that Fay would feel sick and ill the moment that she returned. She had heard her called down to the kitchen, had listened to the sound of voices raised in argument, the vindictive, angry argument that Mrs. Denvers always used; then the sound of a door shutting, and suddenly a girl's piercing screams.

She won't bother me again, thought Eileen, and told herself that she had paid off several old scores.

The screams went on and on. They became rather frightening. Then silence, an even more paralysing silence!

She heard her father come up to bed, and the sound of his throwing off his boots, with a noise that usually woke Doris, but not tonight. There came the sound of the sagging bed as he flung himself on to it.

Then Mrs. Denvers again. Mutterings on the stairs, and the door opening with a chink of yellow light, and the smell of oil and lamp wick and general frowst.

Fay came in, and she seemed to be almost broken in two. She did not undress, but lay down on the mattress with the two children the other side of her. She did not cry. She had gone deathly white, with a whiteness that Eileen suddenly found frightening. She lay there, and her eyes were two dark splotches sunk into caverns—leastways, they looked like caverns to Eileen.

Then she fell asleep.

When she woke again Fay had gone.

Fay had lain there in pain all through the night, quite unable to sleep because whichever way she turned her body throbbed and ached. She could not bear it. It was not only having to suffer that way, and the knowledge that Eileen had done this thing (because she had known that from the first). It was the bitter humiliation of it. The swinging of the pendulum first

this way, then that. She had been a woman at
one moment, a woman in love in the musky
sweetness of that barn, and knowing Noah's
caresses, and strong in her emotional feeling for
him. Then she had come home walking as
though there were no earth beneath her feet
but a new sort of heaven. Instantly it had
changed, so quickly that it left her bewildered,
and she was treated as a child, degraded, and
beaten.

She could not bear it.

She made up her mind in those small hours
when the white moon rose, and the clouds
gradually died away, and the room was full of
starshine, that she would go to the gipsies. She
would go to Noah and throw herself on his
mercy. She hated the thought of the old woman
who had told her fortune, but she believed that
was something that she could suffer because he
would protect her.

When she tried to stir, she could not.

She waited awhile until the dawn came.
Then she knew that if ever she was to make the
effort it must be now. Soon her mother would
be down; she could already hear her moving in
her room. Soon she would be getting the breakfast for her father, and tying up the dinner ready
for him to take to the lambing yards. Eileen

and Doris were asleep, and it was a comfort to Fay to see Eileen's somnolent eyes fast shut.

She levered her body up.

It ached almost worse than last night, and was heavy, like the body of some very old woman.

She got to the window, afraid that she should groan, and she thrust her aching body through the aperture. It was agony slithering down the corrugated iron to the garden below. She thought that she would never survive the final landing, but she did, and picked herself up. Then she started very slowly, because she ached so dreadfully, for the fair ground.

She left the village behind her, climbing the hill painfully. Surely, she thought, they will not turn me out when they see my plight?

Noah she could rely upon, and after all if Haidee would not have them, and as queen she had a perfect right to turn them away, then surely she and Noah could live together under hedges for the summer, and sell the pegs and the brushes and the mats that he made.

The idea was strangely appealing.

Suddenly as she came to the open space beyond the village and the little hill which rose steeply from the river, where a round red brick bridge crossed it, she saw that the fair field was empty. Across its scarred surface there were

only the remains of what had been! A darkness where fires had burned, earth shovelled
back into holes where props had been dug in.
A few stray papers blown hither and thither by
the little wind which comes with the dawn. In
the distance, half a mile away (where she could
not possibly overtake them in her present con-
dition), the last of the vans rolled on rollicking
wheels.

They had gone.

Now she knew that she could not overtake
them, that she could not hope to meet Noah
again for a whole year. She sank down into the
ditch, afraid lest her escape should have been
discovered from home, and her father be sent
after her. She need not have worried herself.
It had not entered their heads that she would
dare to defy them again, and the shepherd was
too busy with the thought of his ewes, and getting away to the lambing yards quickly, to worry
about his daughter.

Mrs. Denvers was full of complaints, and, as
Eileen still slept, the cottage was quite undis-
turbed by any thought of Fay.

She sat in the wet ditch for a while, and
forlornly stared at the world. Here were lords
and ladies, and the first fine ferns of cow's
parsley; here was the scent of primroses and wet

moss, but the earth stained her frock, and she realized that she looked tumbled after sleeping in it all night. She knew that her face was swollen and stained with tears, and that she looked very much like a gipsy herself in this state.

What was she to do?

She dared not go home again, even though her father would have gone, but her mother would be vindictive. The probability was that she would lock Fay in another room, or the out-house, until her father could return to beat her again.

The belt was the only method they knew of enforcing control, and she felt that she would die if he raised that belt against her any more! Already her skin was broken and bruised, and she dared not contemplate her reactions if she had to submit to another beating. Her throat ached with screaming.

She dared not go home.

Yet she had nowhere else to go, because like this she could not apply for a place in service; no lady would look twice at her. She could do nothing to help herself, and she sat there crying weakly.

She thought of James Day.

She did not know why she thought of him,

save that yesterday he had been kind, and had done all in his power to help her. She could not believe that he would turn her willingly from his door, even though she did look like a gipsy girl and even though she did speak croakingly like a rook.

She got up.

She could circumvent the village easily, by going the long way round across the water meadows, and, by this means, no gossips would get the hang of the tale. She knew that if they saw her like this they would be the first to challenge her appearance, and the story would grow. They would say that she was in trouble and that her father had beaten her for it; she did not think that she could bear the chat that would follow.

She crossed the water meadows laboriously, and, when she came to the ford, washed her face in the stream, and dried it on her petticoat. She felt better for that, for the water was icy cold and comforting.

She saw the mill; usually it looked near from where she now stood, but today, because she felt so weak and ill, and sore, it seemed to be a great way off.

On and on she went, growing more tired.

Then she saw James Day come out of his door,

and stand in the porch, with the cart alongside, apparently ready to make off on some journey.

She called to him.

When she heard the sound of her voice she was amazed at it; it was so hoarse, so unlike it usually was, but it bridged the distance and reached him, because he turned and looked at once in her direction.

" It's Fay," she called.

She did not know whether he heard, but he came to the water's edge, and stood there, shielding his eyes from the sun, which had risen now and was flooding the world with gold. He stared at her; apparently he did not recognize this untidy girl who walked so lame.

" Fay," she screamed again.

The word penetrated and he understood what she meant. Instantly he went round to the low bridge, and, crossing it, came to meet her.

She knew that he was staring at her in amazement as though he could not understand what had happened to bring her to this pass. He came closer and, seeing that she was in such a plight, broke into a run. His eyes were anxious.

" Good heavens! what has made you like this? You're ill."

She nodded; now, because she was so weak,

the tears were running down her cheeks, and she did not know what to do. She could not speak.

He did not let her walk, but gathered her up into his arms, holding her across his breast, and carried her like a little child into his home. She shut her eyes, crying weakly, and hid her face in his shoulder. It was an old coat, the coat he wore for milling, and it smelt of wheat and corn, and of dust, but it was very pleasant.

Only once did she glance up and it happened to be the moment that they passed the willow tree, which was sprouting new leaves, and whose twigs were scarlet. It was queer that she should look up then, seeing all that willow tree had meant to James and the tragedy that it had brought into his life.

He went into the house. It was large and comfortable and much better furnished even than the best room in the cottage at home. The floor was red-tiled, and shone as though it were polished. Before the fire was a big sheep-skin rug and a sofa covered in chintz. He laid her down upon it tenderly. Then he brought water and a clean towel, and bathed her face and her hands, and tried to rub the earth stains from her frock where she had lain in the ditch. He was tender as a woman.

"Have you had food?" he asked.

She shook her head. She could not trust herself to speak at this particular moment.

He brought some food from the pantry, which had been a dairy one time, and smelt cool as he opened the door to it. He set on a kettle for tea, and made it with all the care and attention that a woman would have given it. It was obvious that he was well used to fending for himself and that he was capable. He boiled an egg in a small blue enamel saucepan, and made toast, buttering it for her, as though she had been a queen.

"It will make you feel better," he said.

She ate it.

At first she had thought that she would never be able to swallow a single mouthful, but once she had sipped the tea it was easy.

"Now," he said, when she had finished, "tell me what happened."

"It happened last night."

"You haven't been out all night?"

"No," she said—"no, of course not. I got home after the fair, and I had arranged to meet someone in the wooden barn."

"I see."

His eyes looked hurt, but he did not reproach her; she had an idea that he knew about this.

She had to explain. She felt that things had

come to such a pass that she had to tell the truth.

"He was one of the gipsies. I know it sounds awful, but it wasn't awful in real life! He was so kind to me, and he sang so beautifully. He is going with Mr. Richard from the vicarage to have his voice trained. He is going to be really great one of these days, and then he is coming back to marry me."

"You believe that?"

She said, "Of course I believe it. He promised me," quite simply, because she knew it for the truth.

"But these people, these gipsy fellows, they'll promise anything! Theirs is a vagabond life. They wander from place to place, they have no abiding city. Surely you realize that? You can't rely on their promises?"

"I can rely on Noah."

He said: "My poor child, because you are in love with him won't make him any different."

"He will come back. I know he will come back, if only I can wait for him. It's my people. . . ." And she began to cry again, covering her swollen face with her hands, and weeping like a distressed child.

"Listen," he said, "don't cry any more. You will only make yourself really ill, and that won't

do. You are in love with Noah and you want to
marry him?"

"I'll never care for anybody else like I care
for him. I'm going to wait, and next time the
fair comes to the meadow he'll be there and
ready to marry me. He'll be rich then."

He said sympathetically: "My poor child,
don't you think that might not be true?"

She could not bear the thought that Noah
could have deceived her, and turned wretchedly.

"I'd die if I thought that."

"You mustn't die! You must go home."

"No, I couldn't."

"But why not? Is it that you are afraid what
they will say? Haven't you been home for the
night?"

She said: "Yes, yes, I have been home "; then
she began to cry again, for the memory hurt too
much.

"What is the matter?"

"I can never go home again," she confessed.

"Why not?"

"I slept there," she said.

"But your mother and father are the people
to see after you. You are ill. How did you get
into this state?"

She told him, in a little whispering voice because she was so ashamed. She told him, and her

eyes welled with unshed tears as though she could not cry any more.

"My father beat me. I can't go back. He will do it again. I know he will do it again, and I could not bear any more. Don't think me a coward—it isn't that—but I'd die before I went through that humiliation."

James Day looked at her. His mouth was set and his eyes had gone very hard, though never towards her. "My dear," he said, "will you stay here whilst I go and see your mother at home and your father at the lambing yard? This cannot happen. If I make them promise that nothing like this shall ever be again, if I make them promise that they will not even speak harshly to you, will you go back?"

"I don't want to."

"I cannot keep you here. If I did you must know how the gossips would chatter. It would be a glorious chance for them to open their silly mouths."

He was right.

"Yes, I know," she said.

"What do you want to do?"

"I want to earn my living for the year. I could go into service somewhere; it is the job that I do best. Or I could be in a shop. Anything, but I can't stay here."

"No; I do understand that you cannot stay here with your people. I'll try to fix something up for you, but meanwhile home is where you belong."

"I daren't go back."

He said: "If I make them promise first? If I swear that it shall be all right?"

She did not know what to do, but began to cry again. Eventually he made her promise. He treated her like a small child, cajoling and pleasing. In the end she left it in his hands.

He left her lying on the sofa with the promise that she would not leave the premises until he returned, and he knew that he could trust her to keep her word; then he started across the water meadows to interview Mrs. Denvers.

III

Second marriages are the triumph of hope over experience.—DR. JOHNSON.

MRS. DENVERS had discovered Fay's absence the moment she went up to the room.

She shook Eileen awake.

"Where's that baggage of a sister of yours gone off to?"

"I dunno; I was asleep."

"Gone back to that gipsy fellow as like as not.

What shall we do? All the village will be laughing at us. All the people will be gossiping."

She went down the stairs again muttering to
herself. She went to the door and looked out.
Her husband had gone to work and she could
not run after him to the lambing yard to tell him
what had happened. Neither could she trust
anybody else to take the message, seeing that
would mean that the whole village would be set
chattering.

Oh, what'll I do? she asked herself.

The next thing that she knew was that James
Day was walking into her kitchen, and sitting
down on one of the hard wooden chairs, looking
searchingly at her. There was something about
his manner that she did not like, and Mrs.
Denvers wanted to like him. He was the last
man in the world whom she wanted to quarrel
with, seeing that she understood it might be possible for him to marry Fay. Only, as she kept
arguing with herself, what was the good of that
if Fay had disappeared and wasn't there to be
married?

"Good morning," she said, as civilly as she
could when she did not feel in the least civil.

"I came about Fay."

"She's just run up to the farm for some milk,"
said Mrs. Denvers, she thought with admirable

skill. When she told a lie it was always a good
one.

"No, she hasn't. She is at my place."

Mrs. Denvers swallowed hard.

"We've had trouble with that gel," she said,
even though it might spoil all chances with
James, as undoubtedly it would. "She's been
downright naughty. Last night her father had
to give her something to go on with, and she at
her age too! It has fair upset me."

But she didn't look upset.

"It has upset Fay a great deal more. She came
into my house this morning, dragging herself as
though she couldn't walk."

"You don't know what she had been doing."

"I do. She went out with one of those gipsies.
She told me so herself."

"The little cat!"

He said: "Gipsies can be attractive fellows,
you know."

"They're a dirty lot! Anybody knows that."

He said: "I don't agree with you in all you
say, and the question now is what is to be done
about Fay? The gipsies have gone."

"And a good riddance! Fay had better come
back home. Her father'll see to her."

"Fay isn't coming home under any conditions
of that sort."

"She is under age. We can make her come back," said Mrs. Denvers vindictively.

"After a girl is sixteen you cannot make her come back provided she is in a suitable place," said James, "and if there is any more of this, Fay is going to my aunt in the town."

Mrs. Denvers knew what sort of a gossip that would start, and she was one of those people who lived in hourly fear of chatter. She herself was one of the most malicious gossipers in the place; therefore she knew to what limits they could go.

"Fay must come back here," she said.

"Fay must not be knocked about. I suppose you know that her father could be summoned for assault?"

"That's a pack of nonsense."

She had never thought that she would dare to talk to James Day like this, but something had made her very angry. She was furious that Fay should have gone down to the mill, "pitching a tale," as she put it.

"Now, which is it to be?" asked James. "She comes back here, and you behave properly to her, or I take her under my wing."

"You mean marry her?"

She felt that she might as well say what she meant.

James knew quite well that in Fay's present

mood marriage would be impossible. She was in love with Noah and she would stay faithful to him anyhow until the year was up, when she believed that he would come back to her.

"She is too young," he said.

"That's nonsense too! I was married when I was her age."

He glanced at Mrs. Denvers with her tired, strained face, and her body misshapen with child-bearing. He felt suddenly some measure of sympathy for her, for half her trouble came through overwork. She had slaved for this shepherd husband of hers, and had undertaken far more than she could do, with the result that she was continually irritable.

He said: "Surely that has taught you that eighteen is too young to marry? In a year's time, perhaps. Not before."

"You care for my gel?"

"Yes."

Then, she thought quickly, here was the chance to vindicate herself with the neighbours. The girl who married James Day would be lucky. She would have an enviable position as regards the neighbours, which would mean that Mrs. Denvers could hold up her head again.

"In a year's time you want to marry her?"

"If she'll marry me."

So like a man, thought Mrs. Denvers. Fay would marry him right enough, because she'd see to that. " Of course she'll marry you."

James knew that it was useless to go into details of her affection for Noah, because Mrs. Denvers simply would not understand. He couldn't expect it of her.

" Now," said he, " let us consider the present position."

" Maybe we were a bit hasty last night, but it was her father's fault."

" Will you promise not to mention this to Fay if she returns?"

" Oh, I'll promise all right."

He said sternly : " I shall make it my business to know if you break that promise, and don't you forget it. I shall be here to enquire, and if you've frightened her again I shall take her away and send her to my aunt's then and there. What's more, I mean it."

She knew that he meant it.

" Very well," she said, " I promise."

She had weighed up the pros and cons, and knew that there was more to gain by agreeing than refusing. Besides, she realized that she could let Fay know all about it the moment that she got her back under her own care.

James Day had realized that.

He said: "Mind you, I shall hold you to that! You won't doublecross me. If Fay comes back, she comes back to be happy, not to have her father knocking her about, and you taking it out of her with a nagging tongue."

"Oh, what stories she has been telling you!"

"They are not stories. I've seen the girl; she is at my house now, and she is thoroughly broken. I could go further with this, you know. I could have the law on you both for laying a finger on her, and what is more, I will, if there is any more trouble."

She stood there sulkily.

She would have liked to flare up, and to tell him exactly what she thought of his interfering, but there was too much at stake. She wanted everything that he could give her. The kudos of having a daughter at the mill house, the knowledge that there would be pickings, and the joys of having a rich son-in-law.

"There won't be no further trouble," she said.

"Very well."

He turned away and walked up the village, determined not to leave it there. He did not trust Mrs. Denvers with her screwed-up face and her small, hostile eyes. He knew quite well that, given a chance, she would be nagging at Fay worse than ever. James Day was a man's man.

He understood men and had never understood women in the same way.

He passed up the hill with the little houses on either side, and the thatched cottage in the orchard where the buds were swelling on the apple trees, and where soon there would be a sheen of pink and white blossom.

He came to the red farm at the top, built like a doll's house, with three windows above and two on either side of the porch. There were daffies nodding in the two round flower beds set before the windows, the first of the daffies, for this little garden was specially sheltered and hemmed in. The plum tree was in blossom, white stars on the dark boughs, in vigorous contrast.

He passed the cow yard with the gates open to show that the herd had gone back to pasture, milking done. A tall red barn shouldered the road, and he passed along to the rick yard beyond, where there were hurdles plaited with straw and set there for the lambing season.

He could see the shepherd and his boy working there, their heads and shoulders appearing over the straw-plaited hurdles, giving them a curious appearance of having no legs.

"Denvers?" he called.

Denvers came to the rough gate. He held in his arms twin lambs, small, with amazed black faces, and legs and tails idiotically long. He handled them carefully, as though they were precious, as indeed they were, and he had a respect for their infancy and helplessness which James could not associate with his treatment of his own daughter last night.

He said: "I want a word with you."

"A word?"

"It's about that daughter of yours."

"What—Fay? You haven't found her? The blessed gel ran away again this morning, I hear. The wife sent our Jimmy along with a message. That girl'll be bringing trouble on our house, and that's a fact."

"Not so much trouble as your treatment of her is likely to bring on yourself," said James, shortly.

"What do you mean?"

"Don't you know that it is against the law to treat that girl as you have done?"

Denvers did not bluster.

Long ago his wife had knocked any attempt at bluster out of him, and he stood there blinking owlishly, with the sunlight painting golden patterns on his rough coat and the lambs making feeble noises in his arms.

"Your daughter is at the mill with me."

"She ought to come home."

"You have no legal right to compel her. She is old enough to choose for herself, and after your behaviour she will probably stay away."

Denvers did not think of what the village would say; he was much more occupied with what his wife would say. He knew the length of her tongue.

"That's rum!" he said.

"I've been to see your wife. I can persuade the girl to do what is best, and if you are going to treat her properly it would be best for her to come home. But not if this is going on happening. Your wife has given me her word that she will stop nagging. But you know what women are."

Denvers shifted the lambs both into the same arm, and thrust his hat back on his head uneasily.

"Yes, I know what women are."

"You're the head of your home. You are the one legally responsible for what goes on in that home," said James, quite coldly.

"Yes, I suppose I am."

"What's more, I'm holding you responsible. I'm going by no woman's word! The girl fell for this gipsy fellow; she thinks she is in love with him. He has gone. She'll fall out of that mood given time and the chance. You aren't giving her a chance."

Still Denvers stood there looking at him help-lessly, with the little new lambs in his arms.

" Maybe you're right," he said at last.

"I know I'm right! Fay is coming back home, but if there is one mite of trouble she'll come back to me and I'll send her away for a time to my aunt in the town. Then the whole village'll know."

" I see."

" And you understand?"

"Yes," he said, " I understand."

For a moment James lingered, staring him full in the eyes, then he bade him good morning and turned sharply on his heel. As he went up the lane with the lazy day struggling out of the clouds, and the sunshine growing and strength-ening, and the leaves expanding after the rain, he began to whistle.

He thought that he saw daylight at last.

IV

The quality of mercy is not strained,
It droppeth as the gentle rain from Heav'n
Upon the earth beneath.
                              WILLIAM SHAKESPEARE.

FAY came back to the cottage. James brought her that afternoon when she had had time to iron her frock and to let her swollen face go down a little.

Whilst he had gone to the village she had examined the mill house.

She had never been inside it before, and stared about her with curiosity. It was so much better furnished than the cottages in the village. She liked the pictures. James loved beauty. He had not hung upon his walls the peculiar series of pictorial historical events which had attracted the other cottagers. Here was a picture of sun-flowers by Van Gogh, here was a picture of two swans flying over a moor, tattered with long grasses and sedges, and with the sun falling into twilight in the distance. She liked the furniture too, old and smooth to the touch; mellow with time, and much polishing.

Everything was very clean.

She went upstairs because her curiosity could not stay her, and she was struck by the simplicity of the room that he used. It was not over-cluttered with furniture like their own cottage, but the boards were left bare, with vividly coloured mats here and there, striped in tangerine, and black, and jade in vigorous contrast. There was an Oriental blanket across the big double bed, which once he must have shared with poor Violet.

On the dressing-table was a photograph of her. Fay felt sure that it must be a photograph of

her, and went across to look at it. She was very
slight and childish-looking, with fair hair drawn
back, much the same colour as Fay's own hair,
and a little triangle of a face, out of which the
eyes looked to be strangely large and luminous.
There was something odd about that face, she
knew, some disturbed mental balance which she
could not but associate with the willow outside.

Just beyond the window the willow stood.

How can he bear to sleep with that thing just
out there? she thought.

There is no accounting for facts and happen-
ings in life, and she supposed that by now he had
grown so accustomed to the willow that he had
ceased to think about it.

But it gave her a strange feeing as she stood
here, staring into its branches, reaching upwards to the sky and down to the water's edge.
Violet must have been a queer person; she wished
that James had told her more about the way that
she had behaved.

She crossed the landing with the humpy floor,
saw another room with two little beds in it, and
yet another much smaller room, unfurnished
save for a child's cot. The sight of it was like a
ghost.

Then they had a child, she thought, and wondered that she had never heard tell of it in the

village. Nobody had ever said anything about that.

Yet here, in the little bare room with the walls painted a delicate shade of blue, very carefully, as though it were a labour of love, the single cot stood. She went to it. It was a folding cot. Inside it was a blanket of soft wool, and bound with satin—the kind of blanket no miller buys for his child. There was a small lace pillow, with ribbon threaded through it, daintily. She touched it with furtive fingers.

Here was something that she felt to be secret. She stared round the room. In it there were signs of preparation. The walls had been painted with skill, the ceiling had been tinged pale pink. She had never seen a pink ceiling before, and it surprised her. The floor remained as it had always done, unstained wood, with little hills in it as becomes a very old floor.

Yet somebody had fixed the wooden pelmet at the window, half finished it. A board rested against the side waiting to be put up, and on the sill was a screw of paper with some nails in it. They had gone rusty.

All this must have happened a very long time ago if one could judge by the nails, she thought.

The cot itself was clean. Its supports were

painted in shiny blue enamel, its canvas hammock was spotless, and the little blanket and lace pillow were fresh and new. Nothing seemed to fit in together.

She went downstairs again and waited for James to return. When he came back he was smiling.

He said: "I've seen both your father and your mother, and they have promised that there shall be no more of this. If you come home with me no more will be said."

"You don't know Mother."

"I've frightened her. I've frightened her as she deserved, and I think she daren't say very much."

She stared at him helplessly.

"I got a promise from her, but as I was not too sure about it, I went to see your father also. He was at work in the lambing yards, and I told him just what I had told her. They know now that if there is any more of this there'll be real trouble! I've told them that."

"Do you think they'll understand?" she asked, because she was afraid of being left alone with them in that cottage again, and of Eileen, who would take a delight in telling on her, and of the complications they might bring to bear upon her.

"Will you take my word for it? I have an open door here for you. If there is the slightest trouble you can come back here to me?"

Again she said weakly: "You are very good."

Because the caravans had trailed away into the distance, and for the moment Noah had gone out of her life, she knew that she had no option. She had to go back to the cottage.

"But," she said, "you will help me. If I could get some job away? I want to get away, right away for the year."

"Till he comes back?"

"That's it. Till Noah comes back."

James leaned forward.

"What happens if he doesn't come back?" he asked again.

"He will."

She was so much in love that she was prepared to swear by him. She would not entertain the idea that he could do anything but return to her.

"I know he will come back," she said.

"Very well. I will get in touch with my aunt and see what can be arranged. There must be some job you can do in the town. I'll see about it, I promise you."

"I shan't be happy at home."

"No, I understand how you feel. For the

moment you must go home, but I'll do my best
to get you away as soon as I can "; and she knew
that he meant what he said.

It was queer how she asked him, but suddenly
she had the feeling that she must know. She
asked the question without any preliminaries.

" James, did you ever have a child?"

He stared at her. " So you've been exploring
the house? Well, I suppose that's only natural."

" It is a beautiful house."

" I hoped you'd think that."

" But the little room and the cot?" she asked,
watching him.

" No, I never had a child."

" Then . . . ?"

"You wonder why it is there. I'll tell you,
though, mind you, I've never told anybody else.
I thought that we were going to have one.
Violet did not want it. She had a terror of having a baby and she did not care about them
really. I've always loved them."

" Was that," began Fay, " at the time?"

He nodded.

"Yes, that was at the time. I think that was
the beginning of it all. You see, she had a queer
mind. I don't think that I noticed it when I met
her; she was so lovely, so whimsy. I used to
follow her about like a little dog, because at that

time she could do anything with me. I brought
her here, and she had never been in the country
before. She was born in London, you know."

"Yes, I heard that."

"The country worried her. Too quiet. At
first she said that she could hear voices in the
mill stream. 'Listen,' she'd say, 'don't you hear
them calling?' And I'd tell her that it was just
the water. Then I told myself that she wasn't
really strange; it was that she had an imagination
and that she liked to think that she was hearing
the fairies calling her. She said that the willow
was a witch, and looked at her with black eyes.
You know the holes where the boughs have been
lopped? They look very strange and ominous
in winter. She was always frightened of the
witch. I'm afraid I laughed at her. You see, I
did not understand."

Fay said nothing at all.

He said : "I thought it over and I came to the
conclusion that she hadn't really grown up.
She'd been spoilt, you know. So pretty, and so
fascinating with it, that people were inclined to
spoil her. It isn't easy for a girl to grow out of
that sort of thing. I told her that if we had
children it would make a difference. The doctor
thought so too. But she was scared."

"And you never had a child?"

"No. One started to come. Nobody knew about that; it was all so early in the day and it seemed to be so far away. Like a dream, you know. She was worried to death about it. I tried to get her away from that side. I painted the little room, and one day I bought the little cot. She came and looked at it. 'It's pretty,' she said; and then, all queerly: 'What's it for? Is it for a doll?' You see, there were times when she didn't know."

"It was her mind," said Fay.

"Yes, it was her mind, but I was stubborn and wouldn't believe it. I loved her so much, and cared for her, I did not want her to go that way. I believed that the child would make matters very different. Then that day, that very day when it happened. She'd had hysterics. There were times when she used to fling herself down on the sofa and cry there. It was dreadful to see her. I got her round, and I had to go out. It was something that I couldn't afford to miss. I could not leave her that way, so I locked her in her room. Generally she would lie down and sleep deeply and wake up having forgotten that it had ever happened. I thought that it would be like that this time."

She did not know if it would hurt him more to tell her, and stood there helplessly.

At last she said: "Don't . . . don't tell me if it hurts you."

"It isn't that. I think I've been wanting to tell somebody and did not know whom. I came back. The grocer had been and she had called out of the window to him. She was always very plausible—those people are, you know. She called asking him if he would let her out—said she had locked the door and had lost the key. He believed her. He said afterwards that she seemed to be quite natural, just gay and light-hearted as though there was nothing wrong."

"You came home later?"

"Yes, an hour later. She must have got rid of him and come straight down to the willow tree; it was the ghost that she had always said would get her."

"Perhaps it was an accident?"

He shook his head.

"Oh no, it wasn't. She had made dead sure of it. She had gone into the malthouse where I kept the rope, and she had made a proper noose; she must have done it with the one idea, and she had slung it over the big bough, the only one that would hold her. She meant to do it right enough. The awful part was that I found her. If only I could forget that. I want to push it right out of my mind, but it is always there."

"Why do you think she did it?"

"She was frightened to have the child, she was frightened of the future. Her mother went the same way I heard afterwards, because the coroner traced the family in London, and we found that the mother had taken an overdose of something. They couldn't help it, unhappy creatures. Now I think perhaps it is a good thing that the baby never was; it might have been the same, and then what would I have done?"

"It would have been awful."

"It would have been the most terrible thing that could happen to me, and I know it. No, I had a lucky escape. And some day I'm hoping that there will come a time when another woman sits here with me, a woman who is wise, and who does not hear voices in the mill stream nor see the willow as a witch who beckons to her, and looks at her with black eyes. A woman who will give me a child to fill that little cot and live in that little blue room . . ."

He stopped abruptly.

Fay did not know when she had been so moved as she was at this particular moment. For a few seconds she could not speak, but sat there listening to the ticking of the grandfather's clock, and the sound of her own heart, tumultuous and insistent.

Then she said: " I must be going home."

They went home across the water meadows
hand in hand.　There seemed to be no necessity
to talk, but she knew that they understood one
another well.　She was for a moment almost
alarmed that she could love Noah so much, for
she realized that here in James was a man who
could give her such happiness, and could make
her such an excellent husband.

But, she thought quickly, the wheel tracks of
those gipsy vans had ridden through her heart
and had left an impression there.　It was inescapable.　There was no getting away from that.

V

I'll hope no more
For things that will not come;
And if they do, they prove but cumbersome.
Wealth brings much woe,
And, since it fortunes so,
'Tis better to be poor
Than so to abound
As to be drowned
Or overwhelmed with store.
ROBERT HERRICK'S *Prayer*.

FAY'S family received her coldly, because they
were embarrassed by their own action.　Her
mother was offhand; she had not the ability to
carry off a difficult situation with anything save

rudeness. Denvers himself sat back in his windsor chair and read his Sunday paper through and through again, uncomfortably ignoring the fact that his erring daughter had returned.

The trouble with Bert over the poaching was occupying much of their time and discussion, which was a merciful thing.

Only Eileen spoke of it to Fay in their room that night.

"You didn't half cop it," said Eileen. She still felt ill; it had been biliousness owing to the cheap sweets from the fair, and she was one of those children whose insides cannot stand such a menu.

"You shut up!"

"If you say anything to me, I'll yell for Mother, and that'll happen again."

"It *won't*," said Fay firmly.

There was something about the way that she said it which silenced Eileen, so that she turned on her pillow with mutterings and woke Doris, who began to cry. Mrs. Denvers screamed up the stairs:

"Can't you kids be quiet?"

Fay lay awake long into the night. She knew that she could never bear life here, and that she must see James and beg him to get his aunt to help her. She would go to the town, get work in service or in some shop. After that it should be easier.

She did not get a chance to see James until Sunday, when he arrived at the gate in the early afternoon and suggested a walk. This met with Mrs. Denvers' approval because she recognized it as the stage known as "walking out," and liked the idea.

They went for a walk across the water meadows together, where the marsh marigolds were out in brave splotches of colour, and Fay confided in him that, although her people were quite pleasant to her, and there had been made no mention of the incident, she would be far happier if she could get right away. It seemed that he had expected this and had already written to his aunt.

"We'll get something arranged," he said.

Impulsively she told him that she would be afraid to accept the aunt's hospitality because it would seem to tie her to James, when in reality she would be tied to Noah.

"It doesn't matter," he said.

She knew when she came back from that walk that she had loved the time spent with him. She could lean upon him. He was the strong prop in her life, which her people had never been, and she knew that he understood her.

Within a week she had the invitation to go to stay with his aunt.

When this was first mentioned in the Denvers family it caused consternation. Mrs. Denvers had thought that the whole matter was now safely settled, that the past was pleasantly forgotten, and all she had got to do was to settle down looking forward to the time when Fay would marry James satisfactorily. She did not like the idea of the girl going to the town, where, as she said, anything might happen, and in reality the thing she was most afraid of was that the affair might be spoilt. Absence, according to Mrs. Denvers' lights, did not make the heart grow fonder!

However, it was useless beating her head against a blank wall, and she knew it. With a wry face she allowed Fay to go and for the next few months Fay made her home away.

Time slipped by rapidly.

Mrs. Day was a meticulous old lady who lived in a small back street of the town; she was what is known as "better class." The house pertained to being a villa, and here she lived with her dog, one of those large white fox-terriers, over-size and over-sharply tempered, who spent its life at the iron gate growling at passers-by.

Fay liked Mrs. Day, though she realized that

she was a woman she would never get to know any better. She managed to get a job in a baby linen shop, and there she worked quite happily, aware that she could pay her way, and for the time being stand on her own feet. She could save a little too for the time when she would marry Noah, and then she would be able to afford a little trousseau which would be very charming.

The next few months passed in a daze.

At first her feet ached terribly, and she hated the smell of flannels and woollen garments in the closed-in little shop. But she liked the woman she worked with and she would far rather be here than at home in the village with a family who disliked her.

Occasionally James himself came to see her, and was always interested in her stories of how life went on. He had advice to offer; he brought her news of her people, who never seemed to be very anxious to see her. She did go home, it is true, on the August Monday, when there had been an accident with a chaff cutter and little Jimmy had had his hand badly damaged. Her mother seemed to blame her for this accident in some extraordinary manner, and there were words.

It was such an unpleasant afternoon that Fay

made up her mind that she would never return
again, but when she learnt that Mr. Richard was
coming back to the vicarage for Christmas, she
did go to the village. She believed that Mr.
Richard could give her news of Noah, and now,
after these months of silence, she was aching
for it.

She bought presents for the children and a
suitable gift for her parents and arrived at the
cottage on the Christmas eve. Until now she
had not fully realized how uncongenial it would
be to share a bedroom with Eileen and Doris
again. She had not thought of the close quarters
of the cottage, more particularly in the winter-
time when they were herded into the back
kitchen together, all sitting, it seemed, in one
another's laps.

Her mother's tongue was sharper than ever.
She thought that it was high time Fay married
James, and that it was nothing but a pack of nonsense that things had progressed no way since the
spring. You couldn't keep a man hanging about
like that without his expecting more, she said.
Fay held her peace.

She made the excuse that she was going out
carol singing, and went up to the vicarage after
dark. It was a mild winter's night, with a few
stars in the sky, and a risen moon. There was

no frost. She could hear the thin voices of the children carol singing all around her, for it was their one grand chance to make a little extra. She walked quickly and turned in at the vicarage gate, going to the back door and asking to see Mr. Richard.

" Oh, all right; I'll tell him," said the maid, obviously very surprised.

She wondered if it was impertinent of her and if she dared ask the question that rose to her lips. But she must have news of Noah. She could not go on like this, blindly, helplessly, not knowing what would happen to him.

Mr. Richard received her in the vicar's little study hung with sporting photographs of himself in the cricket eleven, or playing hockey at Cambridge. It was a drab little room, she thought.

She said : " I do hope you'll forgive me, but I wanted to know what had happened to Noah."

"You mean the gipsy boy with the magnificent voice?"

"Yes," she said, and then, very quietly : to be very kind, and tremulously she told him more about it. " We meant a lot to one another."

" Well, he is doing very well indeed. We decided to make a great singer of him, and he has gone abroad to Prague to train. That's a surprise for you, isn't it?"

"Prague. Where's that?"

"Well, it is quite a long way off."

She said tremblingly: "Will he ever come back?"

"Yes, of course he'll come back. He'll be rich and famous. The world is going to know of him; you'll find that."

"Yes," she said, and then, very quietly: "That'll be nice."

Mr. Richard patted her shoulder. "Now you cheer up. You can take it from me that if he promised you he would come back, he will come back. He is that sort of a fellow. You're lucky to have attracted him, and I guess he is lucky in you." And he smiled encouragingly.

She went back home again, and now her eyes were set upon the stars and she walked as though she trod upon them. She knew that Noah would come back to her. She knew that she would meet him again and that it would have been worth all that waiting time. She remembered the smell of the hay-sweet barn, and the feel of his lips on her face and neck, and the way that he had looked at her with those big dark eyes of his. Yes, and the way that he had sung to her.

Now the air was sweet with other singing, the thin sound of piping children's voices telling the news of two thousand years ago.

> What Child is this Who laid to rest
> On Mary's lap is sleeping?

But she could walk as though she trod the heights, because she knew that her man would come back to her. She had only to wait for the spring. She had only to wait for the winter to roll by, and the fair to come back to the meadow, and the stirring music of the roundabout to call her. Then she would meet her man again.

VI

> They will ask you " What have you done?"
> Not "Who were your ancestors?"
> The famous veil in the sanctuary
> Is not reverenced by the faithful
> Because it came from the silkworm.
>> SADI, *the Persian poet.*

IT was spring again and the fair was due. Fay had been tempted to give in her notice at the shop, but she had not done this, because some instinct of self-preservation held her back.

She asked for a holiday, and she came to the village. The night before the fair she could hardly contain herself. She could not go to see

James, because in this she felt that he would not
be able to share her delight, and there was something of shame in her heart.

He had been very kind to her, and she felt
guilty in that she could repay it so badly. But
she loved Noah, and she could not marry James
whilst she loved another man this way.

Her mother was highly suspicious, but she
said nothing. The evening before the fair Fay
went up to the ground where some of the shows
had already arrived, but not the gipsies. The
dwarfs were here, running round to get their
tent erected, and the big roundabout was already
in skeleton form. Men were hammering, and
putting things to right. She walked with Jimmy
over the ground, and he was delighted with
everything that he saw.

Then, as they walked through the mild sweet
evening of spring, she saw the vans coming down
the lane, one after the other in formation, with
Haidee leading in her newly painted smart van,
with a wisp of smoke coming from its funnel
chimney.

They're here, she thought, and her heart
seemed to turn over within her, like the clapper
of a bell when the ringers start raising it.

But of course that was nonsense, because he
would not be with the gipsies, but would come

alone, down from London. Nothing would keep him away, she was sure.

For a time she and Jimmy lingered whilst the vans settled down in their corner of the field, and Zilla and Tessa got busy with the hoop-las and the cocoanut shies and the rifle ranges. She saw old Haidee come to her door, smoking the clay pipe and staring out with a lynx-like eye to see that everybody did their job and pulled their weight. She allowed no slacking, and nobody tried to slack when she was looking on.

Tomorrow, thought Fay, and now she believed that she could not bear to wait.

Tomorrow dawned much as it had been last year. A watery day, with the promise of rain in the bright sunrise, and the wind blowing wetly across the hills. But the fair started at midday and she took Jimmy and Doris up to the field, and did the round of it. It would be better tonight, when the flares were lit and the men had finished their work in the fields, and the women took a holiday from their homes. She stood watching the roundabout starting with but a quarter of the passengers, and the few throwers at the hoop-la, and the shooters at the rifle ranges.

She saw Haidee leaning out of her doorway and looking at her. She wondered if she had

recognized who she was, or whether she surveyed
her as though she were merely one of the idle
crowd and a possible candidate for a fortune.
But Haidee never attempted to induce her to go
inside. She stopped other girls.

"Tell your fortune, dearie—tell you about
the man who is coming into your life; he is dark,
and strong, and rich. You've a lucky face,
dearie. . . ."

But not to Fay.

She does know, the girl thought quickly.

He wasn't there.

Now she was singularly impatient to see him,
and she could not bear the time spent in the
cottage. She went to and fro to the field, searching desperately. The crowd thickened. A
shower blew over during the afternoon, then
passed, and the men who had left work came up
to the field, and chanced their luck with the
rings, or a rifle.

He wasn't there.

She searched in every corner. She went on
searching when the flares were lit and the day
was done. Once in the crowd she met Haidee
face to face, and the old gipsy challenged her
with her fine dark eyes.

"Well?" she said.

"I'm looking for him," said Fay, because she

had to tell somebody and had become superstitious believing that this old woman knew, and
was keeping him from her.

" He will not come," said Haidee; "he is
across the seas. He will forget. When he does
come back many moons will have passed, and
you'll be carrying another man's child in your
arms, as I told you. He will return to his own
people; I told you that too. You will not see
him today."

" He promised me," Fay said, and only at this
particular moment did she realize how much she
had pinned her faith on the fair today. She
could not visualize a future that did not hold
him.

Then she thought quickly: He would not be
here on the fair field, where his mother would
see everything, and it would be difficult for him
to meet the other gipsies; he would not be here,
but back down there in the barn where we met
before, and loved and kissed.

The thought set her on her feet again and she
sped down to the village. The dusk was dark
blue. She came to the barn just as it had been a
year ago, with the same horse, and the clanking
of the manger chain, and the pigs snorting in
their yard.

She went to the barn itself.

It seemed to be darker than it had been the last time when she had squeezed herself through the aperture, and had heard him calling to her from the far side amongst the hay. She slipped into it now. It was gloomy, and it frightened her so that she felt to be intensely alone. It was a loneliness that she did not know how to withstand.

If only she could hear his voice again, but there was no reply.

"Noah," she whispered for a second time.

There was the still sweetness of dead grasses, and of cow cake from the cutter in the corner, but silence. He was not here either.

Now she knew that she had begun to cry, and she turned out again into the empty yard with the wet, sweet air blown about it. She could not bear another moment. Then, as she walked to the gate, she heard James's voice and knew that he had followed her.

"My poor sweet, I know what has happened."

"He hasn't come."

He held wide his arms, and because she was so lonely and so unhappy she went to them. They were safe and secure, a staunch barrier from the rest of the world.

"He said if not this year, then next year," she quavered, "but I cannot go on. How can I keep faith with him when everybody tells me that I am silly, and that he will never come back to me?"

"After all," said James, "he is a gipsy, and a gipsy loves the vagabond life; he is not the kind that settles. Haven't you expected too much of him?"

"I loved him so much."

"I know you loved him. I knew, too, that this might happen."

"Mr. Richard says that he is in Prague, but I thought that he would get back. His own mother said that he would not come, and she was right. They were all right, and I was just a fool."

"No, not a fool! Simple. Trusting. You must not belittle yourself."

She sobbed on his shoulder. "What do I do next, James? I feel so hurt. I feel so help-less."

He said tenderly: "Is it too much to ask you to come to the mill and live there? I'd be kind to you, my dear; I wouldn't ask too much. I know that you love him and only care for me. I would not expect love."

She thought how pathetic it was that he could feel like this, and offer so generously of his life expecting such small reward.

" I want time to think," she said.

" You shall have time to think."

She could hear the manger chain chafing, and the pigs snuffling, and see the stars over the great dark prow of the barn, just as it had been a year ago. Only this time it was a different man, and in one way she loved him, and knew that, had she never met Noah, she would not have hesitated for a moment. It was because she had met a sweeter love that this seemed to be insufficient.

As they neared the gate together, he held her hand in his.

" I think that you will come to me soon, perhaps before the roses?" he said.

" I don't know what to think," she answered.

VII

Desire may be dead
and still a man can be
a meeting place for sun and rain
wonder outwaiting pain,
as in a wintery tree.

D. H. LAWRENCE.

THEY were married in late May.

She had watched the gipsy vans trail away out of the fair field when the day was done, and she had known that she could not wait another whole year.   Goaded by Mrs. Denvers, and village gossip which declared that Noah had forgotten her, she went to the mill house and she told James that she wanted to marry him.

Even though this day last year she could have sworn by Noah's word.   Even though Mr. Richard had said that he would keep his promise and come to her.   They did not understand. There was something humiliating about the fact that she had been so ready to fall into his arms, so ready to yield her heart to him, and he so glib with promises.

Perhaps they were all right when they said it was because he had represented something so much outside her own world that she had fallen so hurriedly in love.   She did not want to think about it.

"I'll marry you, James. I want to marry you," she said.

"I'm a proud man," he answered.

"When is it to be?"

"It can't be too soon for me."

So they arranged it for late May, and although she wanted it to be a quiet wedding, the family were all for having an affair.   A white gown like a May Queen, and a wreath of blossom.   Eileen and Doris to follow her.

"I don't want it that way, Mother."

Her mother turned on her snappily.

"Do you want people to think that there is some reason for keeping it all so quiet?" she demanded.

Fay left it at that.

A week before the wedding she searched the papers desperately to see if in the entertainment world there was some sign of Noah. There was nothing! She even went up to call on the vicar to ask if Mr. Richard had said anything, but the vicar was always of an opinion that the entertainment world was a little revolting, and that it was a shame that Richard should have made all this money out of it.

So her wedding morning came, and Fay went to church in a daze and a white frock, with blossom in her hair.

The villagers clustered together in the churchyard, for there had been talk enough, and there was more talk here on the day that she was actually marrying.

"I wouldn't like to be her, and go to a house as was haunted by a ghost."

"That tree, you know! And the woman who hanged herself on it. It'd scare me."

"And what'd happen if her gipsy boy did come back? They're pretty ready with a knife. You never know, do you?"

The whole thing passed in a daze. It was something that Fay would never remember, for her eyes seemed to have gone blind and her ears deaf. Long afterwards she found herself sitting on the sofa in the mill house, where she had sat that other time. Only now her frock was not stained from the earth of some ditch; it was her white wedding frock, and on her hair were the flowers.

James said: "Don't be afraid."

"I'm only afraid that I have done the wrong thing. Only afraid that, after all, Noah may come back to me."

"Supposing I promise you that if he should I would give you to him; would that help?"

"You couldn't."

"I am so certain that he will never return, so sure that he has forgotten, that I would pledge that and keep to it."

"Maybe you're right. You know the world better than I do."

She stared round the comfortable little room, and she knew that she had done well for herself. This would be no gipsy's life, but a happy life with him. She could rely on James. He would never speak harsh words, nor would he turn an angry hand against her. He was the best man in the parish; had not the vicar said so this very afternoon in his address after he had married them? She could remember that much.

She was lucky. It was only that having met Noah first she could not forget him.

"Then that's a bargain, is it?" she asked, and actually laughed.

"I give you my hand on it."

They ate a meal together. He would not let her do a thing towards getting it, but brought it in himself. Strong, bitter tea, and a cake with white icing on it. They sat there talking over the fire which he had stacked with pine cones, for the evenings were cold. When she went up to bed, to the room with the Oriental mats and the blanket with the pattern of tangerine and black and jade, she could hear the wind rushing through the willow tree, now in full leaf. She felt apprehensive. Of course there was nothing in the village talk that the girl who had died there still stood there at night and called and moaned.

It was idle chatter.

I've done the right thing, she told herself, the only thing that I could do. Pride would not have let me wait any longer for him, and I do care for James.

She must not look back.

VIII

And the Spring comes again
With blossom on the bough
And the green leaf, and the lark singing,
And cuckoo smocks in the lane,
And life is young again,
And new.
And in love.

Anon.

ONE whole year and she had been tremendously happy with James. She had done the right thing. She wanted to make him happy more than anything else in the world, to repay his goodness to her, and his thoughtfulness for her, and his love.

He had fetched and carried for her, waiting on her all the time almost as though she were a lady. She had never thought that a man could be so good to her.

Yet, as the second year of the fair came round, she knew that she chafed, and was restless, and that sometimes she snapped at him in a way that reminded her of her mother and made her afraid. She was nervous. Last year she had been longing for this moment when the vans would return into the field for the fair, and when there might be the chance of seeing Noah. But now she was not longing; she was afraid lest he might come back.

If he did she could not bear it because she would be torn both ways, the way of the man she loved and the way of the man that she had married.

Besides, there was a child coming.

She had hoped that she would not have a child, for she had been afraid this would cement the bond so closely that she could not hope to sever it. It meant that deep down within her there was still the longing for Noah and his love, a beacon, burning bright and unflickering; the knowledge that if he did come back she would want him and would turn to him, and she could not forget that.

Not that, not that, she kept telling herself.

But if there were a child, how could she desert it? It would make the bond stronger. It would make the parting so much more impossible.

The fair came on a magnificently fine day, and this time she did not go to it, excusing herself because of the coming child.

Only at night, when James had had to go to the town on an urgent message, she crept out into the lane, and went again to the barn with the smell of hay. She could not keep away from it. She peered inside the doors, but it was all dark and silent. There was no stirring of the hay, no voice to welcome her.

He had not come back.

In one sense it was an enormous relief. She turned, tremendously satisfied, and now she knew that she could go on with her life, and be happy with her child, because it would mean that the village had been right, and that the world had known better than she did. He had been only playing, his love had been as vagabond as his life, he would not come back to her at all.

In June the child was born, a boy two pounds more than the average weight, a fine fellow with thick, chubby arms, and a face so ridiculously like his father's that it made Fay laugh to see him.

"Here is a son for the little cot," she told James when he came to her room and stood there looking down at them both. He had wanted a boy.

He said: "I can't believe it. It is something almost too much to believe."

"It's true."

It was strange that she did not feel ill, but well, and amazingly happy, as though she had fulfilled her destiny and had repaid James in the way she wanted most to repay him. She was intensely proud.

She lay in that room for a fortnight, happy with her child, happy in her husband's joy.

When she got about again, she felt weak and ailing, but it passed, and she told herself that next year it would be a daughter, a girl with her own ash-blonde hair and blue eyes.

Now she knew that the willow tree which stood beside the door did not worry her any more. The ghost and her baby had passed out of the house for ever; they had, it seemed, been hanged twice over on that tree, and she could afford to forget them.

It seemed that the village felt the same way, for with the new baby at the mill they took it that the old story was dead, and that now the ghost of Violet was laid. Even the children, who had been frightened and had walked all the way round the tree on their way back from school, came sometimes and swung on the low branches.

It was no longer tabu.

And I don't love Noah any more, she told herself; that feeling was something too bright to live.

Only deep in her heart she knew that was a lie.

She knew that although she might keep repeating it to herself a thousand times, there would always be underlying it the knowledge that Noah had stirred in her something that James could never stir.

She was very happy with her son. She was

very happy with her husband. Almost immediately there came the promise of the daughter.

"I had hoped that it would not be so soon,"
she told James.

"Why not? We are young, and we love children. It will be good for the boy to have a sister
at once. They'll be grand playfellows a bit
later."

"I know, but I had hoped . . ." Her voice
trailed off wistfully. Why had she hoped? She
trusted that he did not know the answer. Two
children would chain her irrevocably, they
would be inescapable, and all the time that she
was living here in comfort at the mill her heart
was crossing the country in a van with tottery
wheels. Craziness, of course, a madness she
would have condemned in others, but it stood
for something sweeter than madness in herself.

"You're not still thinking of him?" asked
James.

"No," she said, "no, of course not," and
hated the fact that she had to lie about it. But
she could not admit, after all his goodness and
kindness to her, she was still hungering for a
vagabond.

She was in bed with little Judith when the fair
came again. She could hear the faint noise of
the roundabout coming down into the valley,

for the wind was that way. She could hear the strident music and the screams of laughter from the people in the swing boats. But she knew that he wouldn't be there.

Only today the vicar had brought a bundle of papers down for her to read.

"There is something that might interest you here," he said; he had never been noted for his tact, and he had genuinely thought that she would be interested.

She had unrolled the papers and had read them with horror, and with a torturing love at the same moment. The two combined into something quite uncontrollable within her.

A new musical show had come to the Royal Theatre in the Strand, and it was heralded with approbation by the critics. There was an outstanding star. Here was a man whose voice was real music, a gipsy so they said, with a romantic past behind him. He had been discovered when travelling with the vans at some local fair, had been brought to London and his voice trained. He had studied abroad under the greatest professors, and here he was today the finished object. A second Caruso.

Their only complaint was that he was too good for the rôle that he was playing.

There on the printed page she could see Noah

looking up at her. A little older, a little more polished, but Noah for all that. They had not changed the cut of his hair in that dark, curly mop. Nobody could change the way that he looked with wistful eyes, and the little whimsical twist to his mouth. There he was in the dress that he wore in the play, a gipsy dress, much as she had first seen him.

Until this was brought to her notice she had honestly believed that she could forget. Given time and James's love, and the care of the two children, she could forget him, but now she knew that was just imagination, something that she could not possibly get over. She loved him as much today as she had done when he had sat in the barn with her.

Then she asked herself why had he not come back to claim her? She read the story in the papers. He had been abroad, he had not been able to get back.

Had he not said to her, "Wait! Wait and I will come to you?" She had not waited.

She looked at the child sleeping in her arms, and she thought helplessly how she was tied. But these ties were not strong enough! She would break them to go to him, if only he still wanted her.

Then she remembered Violet, the ghost who

swung out into silence in the green arms of the willow tree, and she knew that James would not be able to bear a second tragedy. He had been so generous in telling her that if Noah came back for her she could go, but she couldn't go really. It would hurt him too much.

What can I do? she asked herself.

She got up that day for the first time, and her legs were trembly, and her heart made a noise.

"It's weakness," said the nurse.

It wasn't only that. She had not felt so ill with the boy.

All day she swung to and fro in a haze of doubt. Would Noah come for her, or had he forgotten? The show had been on a week. She did not know what to say about it. She showed James the pictures when he came in from work, and he looked at them in silence, turning them over one after the other on his lap.

"He's done well for himself," he said after a time.

"Yes."

"He must be very clever."

Again she said "Yes," because she did not know what else she could say.

She knew now, at this particular moment, that she felt as though she had been betrayed. All along she had kept on priming herself in the belief that Noah had not forgotten her. Now she knew that he must have done. He was back in London. He was not away across the seas as he had been last year when the fair came back to the meadow. This time he could have come to her.

" Perhaps he did," said James slowly.

"You mean . . . ?"

"You were in bed with Judith; perhaps he did come back."

She knew that was not true. It was so good of James to try to comfort her, so tender of him, and few men would have been as generous to a rival, but Noah had not come back for her. He would never have been content just to wait in vain; he would have asked of the village folks and they would have told him that she was in the mill house.

" He didn't come," she said.

James said nothing, but sat there with his son in his arms, fondling him and stroking the small, firm legs tenderly. She knew that his eyes had gone dark and full of pain like a dog she had once seen which had been run over. She hated the thought of that.

"It doesn't matter," she said at last. "Why should I worry? I've got the best husband in the world and two most lovely children. Everybody says that they are lovely children. It doesn't matter."

But she knew that these were mere words, for she ached to hear the sound of Noah singing again, the song echoing through the valley; she wanted to hear him coming towards her, and to see those same dark, lovely eyes which now looked up at her from a page.

" You're a dear girl," said James slowly.

She thought: Bit by bit and day by day I'll forget. I'll forget and learn to love James as I loved Noah. I'll forget and then the world will be different and I'll feel better about things.

" We're very happy," she whispered.

He came closer to her and put an arm round her. "You've made me the happiest man in all the world," he said.

" You've been wonderful to me."

No woman ever had a better or more considerate husband, and she knew it. No woman.

In time, she promised herself, in time all this will change. I've got him, I've got the children. And she believed that if she kept on saying it to herself she would eventually believe it.

IX

The little cares that fretted me
    I lost them yesterday.
Among the clover-scented grass,
Among the new-mown hay,
Among the huskings of the corn
Where drowsy poppies nod,
Where ill thoughts gie,
And good are born,
Out in the fields of God.
    ELIZABETH BARRETT BROWNING.

IT was curious that all through that spring Fay should have the feeling that this was not living life, but waiting for something to happen, a passing of time, an epoch between two events. The roses came and went and hung in their sweet clusters about the face of the mill house. The boy learnt to walk, and his sister learnt to smile. Both of them were lovely children, one like the father, the other like the mother. She was intensely proud of them.

She knew that James was proud of them too, but she had the feeling that he realized that something was amiss, and was conscious of this curious feeling of epoch between events, the waiting for some crisis.

It came.

It was a very hot August day, when the house

seemed to be sweltering. She felt that she could not bear it much longer, and she came out into the garden and sat beside the water's edge, with the loosestrife growing in purple spirals, and the rosebay willow herb, and the little close forget-me-nots by the flood gates.

James was away. He had had a call from the town, a call that they had really been expecting. In the spring his aunt had been taken ill, so that she had never seen little Judith. She must have had a stroke, although the doctors never said so, but she had been moved into hospital and there she had lain, unable to do much for herself for some weeks. The authorities had warned James that at any time they might be sending for him. It was quite true that the aunt could go on for many months; she might even get better enough to be up and about again. At the same time the end was in sight; it must come before a year was over.

All through the spring and early summer they had written to her, and James had been occasionally to see her. Fay had sent boxes of flowers from the garden to comfort her, and they had done everything that they could to make the illness a little more bearable.

First thing this morning a telegram had arrived to say that she had had another turn and would he please go at once if he wished to see her alive.

"I may not be back tonight," he told Fay last thing as he gathered his clothes together.

"I'll be all right."

"Get Eileen in to sleep with you."

"No, thank you," she said, and laughed.

She and the boy waved him away. She was not afraid and would not mind being here alone. But now, with the sultriness of the overhanging afternoon, she had suddenly felt that she must have air, and had brought the children out to the water's edge. It was cooler here. There were rings on the surface where the fish jumped, every now and again a swallow swooped and dipped his wings; it was very pleasant.

She sat there almost dozing, with Judith asleep in her arms, and the boy playing with some little stones and making belief that he was building a house.

Then suddenly she heard the sound of a man singing. It was the same sound that she had heard that night when her whole life had changed in the dimness of the barn. The song was ten thousand times more beautiful than it had been then; it caught the echoes, and trilled like the lark. It was life.

Instantly everything in her became alert. She

sat up, almost waking the child, who stirred uneasily as though she scented trouble. Fay scrambled to her feet, and as she did so she must have knocked down the little house of stones that the boy was building, because he screamed to her. She hardly noticed him. She put out a hand and lifted him on to his feet beside her, and together the three of them went to the gate.

The sound of the singing came up beside the water and she saw Noah walking. He had taken off his coat and had laid it over his arm. He was bare-headed to the sun, but it could not penetrate that thick dark hair. He walked as she remembered, loose-limbed and easily, and she could see that the shirt he wore was fine and blue like the skies, and that he wore beautiful clothes.

Nearer and nearer he came, and now she realized that she had always loved him dearly, and that nothing she had ever felt for James could come near this strong, passionate emotion for Noah. She stood quite still.

He came along the path singing, and must have seen her, but he made no gesture. He came closer and to the very gate and stopped.

"I am here," he said.

It was curious that her first greeting should be a reproach. "Why did not you come when you said you would? Why did not you come before?"

"I came the moment that I could"; and then, as he glanced at the boy placidly sucking his thumb and the girl asleep in her arms: "You did not wait?".

"None of this matters," she said; and she indicated the mill with the sun gleaming on it, and the open door with the glimpse of the room that once she had thought so fine inside, and the flowers in the garden. "I married James Day. It was no good, I couldn't go on as I was doing. My people, you know! Oh, you don't know what happened, how difficult it all was, nor how good he has been. He took me away when my father beat me. He sent me to his aunt in the town. What else could I do when you didn't come and when I thought that you had forgotten me?"

"I was away," he said.

"I heard that after. Mr. Richard told me. He said that you were in Prague."

He nodded.

"I have been far and learnt much." But still he was staring at the child sleeping in her arms. She wondered if he would notice that her slim figure was more mature, if he would see that she had changed from girl to woman. She did not want him to notice these things.

"Listen," he said, "I had to come back."

"I know. You have come for me at last." For a moment her voice rang with enthusiasm. "You have come for me, and I am ready."

"You have a good husband?"

"He is wonderful, but he will understand."

"You love your children?"

"Yes," she said, "I do love my children," and was conscious of the pleasant warmth of the baby in her arms, and of the clinging hand of the boy.

"You could not leave all this?" Noah challenged her, and she remembered how searching his eyes had always been.

"I could. I care for you so much. Oh, Noah, I have wanted you."

He said: "I know. I wanted you too. But listen, my heart. I am a vagabond; I wander upon the face of the earth, and my place is eventually with the vans again, in Haidee's place, ruling my people. The gipsies do not like a gold-haired queen."

In the sunshine that hair shone like the corn which was turning to amber on the hillside. She put up her hand and smoothed it. "You don't mean you don't want me?"

He leaned over the gate. "My sweet, I came to see how life had served you. It has served me well. But I tell you I am only a vagabond; I tell you I should make no woman a good husband. There have been other girls, you know. Those girls in Prague were lovely. The fräuleins in Munich where I studied were responsive to me. I am every girl's man, not one girl's man. I am glad that you did not stay faithful to me."

She said quickly: "I don't believe it; it isn't true."

"It is true enough, my dear. I came only to see, not to take you back with me."

She started back a little as though he had struck her. She could have sworn that he would never do a thing like this; she could have been quite sure that he would not treat her so. She saw suddenly the background of home and security, she felt the clinging of the children and knew that if she left them they would be like vines from which the prop is taken, and which fall straggling upon the face of the earth.

"You did not come back for me?"

"No, my sweet, to satisfy my eyes; and they are very satisfied, for you are a lovely woman!"

"Please don't," she said abruptly.

"Your husband is fortunate, and you are lucky too. You would not have been so lucky if I had come back as once we thought I should."

She said suddenly and desperately: "They all warned me that the gipsies are no good."

"They warned you very truly."

She said: "Noah, Noah, why have you changed so much? Why have you changed?"

"Life," he answered, "life is like that; it does not stay still. Life goes on."

He turned and walked away. She watched him go, and all the emotions that she had believed were live and vigorous seemed to die as she stood there. She did not hear James drive up; his aunt had died before he got there, and he had come back quickly because he did not want to leave Fay alone, in case she became afraid.

"My sweet, my sweet, what is it?" he asked.

She turned and fled to him. He took her into his arms to quiet her sobbing, with the children on the other arm. "Hush, my dear; you'll frighten them. What happened?"

They went indoors together, and she clung to him; all he could gather was that she loved him and wanted him to stay with her for ever. Things were going to be different, she said; she did not think that she could go on this way any more.

"No more," she sobbed.

If he understood he said nothing, only wiped her tears away and kissed her tenderly.

"The future is always ours," he whispered. "Take heart, my dear, and don't be so troubled."

"You're so good to me, James. I have never appreciated you half enough."

"That's silly."

"I have never felt that you were the only one; he was always here, a shadow, a ghost, something I could not quite understand. But he has gone now, and for ever. He has gone right away."

"I'm so glad," James whispered.

Noah was pursuing his way along the path over the water meadows. He was rich, he was famous, he had everything that he could want, and nobody could rob him of his exquisite voice. That was a wife who would never leave him widowed.

He went slowly, and he knew that the heart which had been so light as he came this way was now heavy and dark. He knew that now his road must end with the van where he had been born and that, however great he might be, and famous, and rich, he would go back to the yellow wheels rotating down the lanes, and to the mother who had predicted this for him in her crystal.

In his pocket his hands fumbled with the

brown berry-like beads of the rosary which he had had as a boy in Austria. It was comfort.

Because this had been his goal. This had been the peak of the mountain, and he had never thought that she would not wait for him. He had studied hard, had worked hard, and the moment that he had the world at his feet had come back to her as he had promised he would do. He had thought of this all the time, this moment when he would take her as a groom takes a bride.

And when he had come for her she stood at another man's gate with his children in her arms.

To Noah time had not passed so swiftly. He had worked so hard that he had had no time to think of anything outside. For there had been no other women for him, there had been no gaiety, no fun, none of the things that he had told her. They had been brave lies.

She is happy here, he had thought; she has married a good man, and she has her children.

He could have taken her with him so easily, but in the end she would have fretted, as all women fret for the flesh which is their flesh, and the blood which is their blood.

No, the brave lie had been the kinder way out; she was happier here. So he had turned away and had known that he had made her hate him, and that his own heart was breaking, just as his mother had said.

He walked towards the sun; he heard the birds singing and the sound of a cutter in the bean fields. The essence came to him sweetly on the air. And, as he walked, he began to sing. My voice is my wife, he told himself; it is now for my voice and my voice alone that I will live.

He went forward.